MW00914978

JESSICA BECK

THE DONUT MYSTERIES, BOOK 35

COCOA CRUSH

The First Time Ever Published!

The 35th Donut Mystery.

Jessica Beck is the *New York Times* Bestselling Author of the
Donut Mysteries, the Classic Diner Mysteries, the Ghost
Cat Cozy Mysteries, and the Cast Iron Cooking Mysteries.

For P & E,
Always!

When Suzanne and Jake leave town to attend a party with friends, they never dream that they are about to become involved in another murder. The stakes continue to rise as an ice storm knocks out the power in the penthouse where they are staying, locking them in with a dead body and a killer until law and order—as well as the power—can be restored.

CHAPTER 1

I FELT JUST LIKE CINDERELLA AS my husband, Jake, escorted me into the massive formal dining room of the penthouse where we were spending the weekend. Gone were my usual blue jeans, T-shirt, and ponytail. Instead, I was wearing an elegant blue gown Momma had bought for me, my hair was styled as tastefully as I could manage it, and though Jake's tuxedo was a rental, he looked better than any movie star to me in it.

It was the height of elegance and sophistication for a gal who normally spent her time toiling away in a donut shop, covered in flour and smelling like yesterday's treats, and absolutely nothing could ruin it.

At least that's what I thought until I heard a woman screaming from the back of the room as we walked in.

Apparently my dream was about to turn into a nightmare.

CHAPTER 2

Two Weeks Earlier

"HI, SUZANNE," A BRIGHT AND chipper voice said one morning, calling my name at the donut shop. It was vaguely familiar, but I couldn't immediately place it, since I had my back turned to my customers at Donut Hearts as I grabbed the last apple fritter for Lincoln Masters.

"Hey yourself," I said without turning around. "I'll be right with you."

As I delivered the apple fritter, I glanced over at who had just greeted me. I had to do a double take when I saw who it was. Not only was I surprised to see the woman in my donut shop without notice, but her demeanor was much different from the last time I'd seen her. Elizabeth Martin was the member of our book club who loved contacting authors over the Internet, but lately she'd lost interest in even doing that.

"Elizabeth? I haven't seen you in ages. You look terrific!" It wasn't something I'd normally say as a greeting to a customer, but my friend looked amazing. The last time I'd seen her, she'd appeared to be on the edge of a nervous breakdown, and I'd been worried sick about her. Her marriage had sounded as though it was in terrible trouble, and she was beside herself with grief. Something had surely changed in the interim. The woman

2

standing before me now looked ten years younger and eight pounds lighter.

"Thanks," she said, blushing a little at my praise. "The truth is, I feel terrific, and I just had to come by and thank you for your advice. You've really been a wonderful friend to me."

"I'm sure you're being too kind," I said. As I recalled our last chat, I remembered that I'd refrained from offering her any specific advice. Only two people really ever knew what was going on in a marriage, and those were the folks who'd taken the vows to each other. Instead, I'd done my best to support her in a troubling time and to let her know that I was there for her if she needed me. "How was your trip with the girls?"

"It was wonderful on so many levels," Elizabeth said, her smile suddenly brightening my shop. "Hazel and Jennifer spoiled me rotten for two solid weeks, and it was exactly what I needed. The best part of it was that when I came back home, Jason was a changed man. I was about to tell him that I wasn't going to keep putting up with his behavior when he started crying! He knew that he'd been neglectful of me, that he had put too much into his business and not enough into us, and that my going away had been a wake-up call for him."

The last time we'd spoken, Elizabeth had confided in me that she'd been worried that her husband had been having an affair. Had she been right about her suspicions? Or had his neglect just been because of his obsession with his business, as he'd told her? I was certainly curious about the answer, but I wasn't about to ask her the question. My friend was happy, and for the moment, that was all that counted for me. "I'm so glad you're working things out. How about that bear claw now?" That had been about all I'd been able to offer her before, but my offer still stood.

"You remembered!"

"Of course I did," I said.

She pondered my suggestion for a second before she responded. "Thanks, but I'd better not. I've decided to drop a few pounds. Not for Jason, though," she quickly added. "For me."

"Well, you look marvelous," I said. "I'm so glad you came by the donut shop. I was so worried about you."

"I know, and I appreciate it. I didn't come by just to update you, though. Here. This is for you."

Elizabeth handed me a cream-colored envelope, and as I opened it, she looked at me expectantly. "What is it?" I asked her.

"Just read it. You'll see," Elizabeth said, grinning.

I pulled out the embossed card and read,

"You and a guest are cordially invited to a formal soiree being held on the weekend of the 17th of this month. It will include three days of fun, fine dining, and friendship, and your presence is most heartily requested. The attire is formal, the dining top notch, and the fellowship we share will be unforgettable."

"There's no RSVP card," Elizabeth said with a grin. "I'm going to stand right here until I get a yes from you. I know it's short notice, Suzanne, but I won't take no for an answer. You can turn Donut Hearts over to your assistant for three days. Please say yes. Jennifer and Hazel have already agreed, and so have my other guests."

"It's tempting, but I really have to talk to Jake first," I said.

"I understand completely," Elizabeth said with a grin. "Go ahead and call him. I'll wait."

"Right now?" I asked, smiling in return. Her enthusiasm was infectious, and I was catching it. "I've got customers. Can't it wait until I close the shop?"

"It can take as long as it needs to take," she said as she stepped to one side. "I'm not going anywhere. There's nowhere else I need to be this morning."

"Okay," I said. As I waited on a few more customers, I pondered Elizabeth's offer. Jake and I weren't normally people who enjoyed formal occasions, but Elizabeth was a good friend, and besides, it could be fun to get away. At least I could ask him to see what he thought. When there was no one else in line, I pulled out my phone and dialed home. "Hey, Jake."

"Yes," he said with a chuckle as soon as he heard my voice.

"Are you agreeing with me that Jake is really your name?" I asked him.

"No, I'm saying yes, we should go to Elizabeth's party," he said.

I looked at my friend and saw that she was grinning. To Jake, I said, "I'm guessing she already spoke with you."

"She came by here first thing this morning, and I've been sitting here waiting for your call ever since. Suzanne, if you're game, then I am, too. We could use a break from our everyday life, you know?"

"I couldn't agree with you more." In a more serious tone of voice, I added, "You're going to have to rent a tux. You know that, don't you?"

"Elizabeth's already taken care of everything. I'm guessing that she's still standing right there waiting for an answer, isn't she? She told me if you resisted, she wasn't going to leave until she wore you down."

"She's here," I answered, smiling at my friend as I replied.

"So, are we going?" he asked.

"If it's okay with you," I answered.

"I'm in," he replied. I could hear the smile in his voice, and then he hung up.

"You actually went by to see my husband before you spoke with me?" I asked her, smiling.

"I decided the best way to approach him was to invite him in person. I hope that's okay with you," Elizabeth replied as a little doubt crept into her voice.

"It's perfect," I said as I stepped around the counter and hugged her. "Jake and I would be delighted to attend."

"I'm so glad!" she said loudly enough to garner a little attention from some of my customers at Donut Hearts.

"There's one condition, though," I reminded her.

"What's that?"

"Emma and Sharon have to be able to step in."

Elizabeth suddenly looked guilty at the mention of their names. "About that."

"They've already agreed to do it, haven't they?" I asked her as I stared into her eyes intently.

"Yes. I'm beginning to realize that I shouldn't have gone around behind your back before I invited you. I'm sorry."

"Don't be. The truth is, it sounds like great fun."

And so it did, at least at the time.

Later events would prove that to be wrong, but I certainly didn't know it at the time.

"Suzanne, I've got great news. You're off the hook," Barton Gleason said a little later when he walked into Donut Hearts. The young hospital chef, who happened to be my assistant, Emma Blake's, boyfriend, was grinning from ear to ear. Was this my day to be surrounded with happy people?

"Excellent," I said, returning his smile. "I didn't even realize that I was *on* the hook."

"About my restaurant, I mean," he said with a grin that intensified. The rail-thin young man was perpetually in need of a haircut, but his smile was infectious.

Some time ago, he and Emma had approached me about the possibility of Barton using Donut Hearts in the afternoon and evening for a start-up restaurant when I wasn't there making donuts. I'd given it some thought since they'd first suggested the idea, but the truth was that I was still on the fence about the proposition. I couldn't deny that the extra money he'd be paying for the privilege would certainly come in handy. Then again, I wasn't crazy about sharing my space, though I figured that was something I could eventually get used to. "I've been meaning to make a decision," I apologized. "Things have just been so crazy lately." That was true enough. Then again, when were things *not* hectic for me?

"I just appreciate the fact that you were willing to think about it. A restaurant in Union Square shut down, so I'm going to give it a go there."

My mind immediately jumped to my favorite Italian eatery and my friends, Angelica DeAngelis and her lovely daughters. "It's not Napoli's, is it?"

"Oh, no. They are an institution. Someone outfitted an empty building on the edge of town nine months ago with a full kitchen, a proper dining room, and everything. They decided after two weeks of being open that the restaurant business wasn't for them, and I got a sweet deal on a one-year lease, since it's been sitting empty and unused since then." He grinned sheepishly. "Just between us, it took every dime I had, but I'm going to make this work. I just turned in my notice at the hospital, so there's no going back now." Barton worked as the chef at our local hospital cafeteria, and I knew that if he changed his mind or things didn't go well, they'd take him back in a heartbeat. People came from miles around to eat at the cafeteria, whether they had to be at the hospital or not. He was just that good.

"I'm really excited for you," I said. I was also worried about the commitment he'd just made, but I wasn't about to bring that up. There was no reason to try to temper his enthusiasm. Besides, if he couldn't be excited going into the venture, he shouldn't do it in the first place. "Is there anything I can do to help?"

"You can lend me Emma for two weeks after you get back from your big party," he said after hesitating for a few moments.

"Does *everyone* in town know my business before I do?" I asked him. "I just found out that I was going myself."

"Your book-club friend doesn't waste any time. She spoke with Emma last night while I was there," he said. "What do you say? I know it will be tough, but it's really important to me."

It would mean two weeks of working seven days a week alone, a prospect I wasn't particularly looking forward to, but he was my friend, so I'd find a way to get through it. "Okay."

"Great. Sharon is willing to fill in for Emma while she's gone, if you want her," he said. "I probably should have mentioned that, shouldn't I?"

The idea of having Emma's mother working in the kitchen beside me immediately took the sting out of my assistant's absence, but then another, darker thought presented itself. "She *is* planning on coming back, isn't she?" I asked him softly.

"I won't lie to you," Barton said in a serious tone. "I asked her to come to work with me full time, but she's loyal to you beyond all belief," he answered with a grin. "All I could get her to agree to was two weeks. The fact is that she has no interest in leaving this place, Suzanne. You two are family."

I had hoped that it was true, but it was still a relief to hear him say it. I knew deep down that I could run Donut Hearts without Emma, but it wasn't anything I particularly wanted to do. She'd left me once before to try her hand at college, but she'd soon come back to the fold. The truth was that Emma was as much a part of my life as the shop itself was. "Good. I'm glad that's settled."

"So am I. Now I'm off. I've got to hit the restaurant-supply store in Charlotte."

"I thought you said that the kitchen in your new place was fully outfitted," I said.

"It is, but there are a few things I've had my eye on since I went to culinary school, and I've just been looking for an excuse to buy them."

I knew the store in question he was talking about, and how high their prices tended to be. "Would you like a piece of unsolicited advice, worth every penny it costs you?" I asked him lightly.

"I'll take all of it I can get from you," Barton said seriously.

"Don't spend a dime you don't have to. If you can make do with what's already there, try doing that first. Then, if there's something you *have* to have, and not just want, think about buying it. I know how marvelous your food is, and I'm not worried about that end of it, but the financial aspects of running a restaurant are ten times harder than keeping a donut shop afloat, and there are times that I'm overwhelmed here."

Barton thought about it for a few heartbeats, and then he nodded. "Okay. That's sound advice. Thanks."

As he started to leave, I asked him, "Don't you want to see Emma while you're here?"

"No, that's okay. We'll have plenty of time to catch up later. Besides, I think she wants to talk to you," he said with a grin as he pointed to the kitchen door, which was clearly open a crack. Evidently she'd been listening in to our conversation the entire time.

"Remember, I'm here if you need me," I said.

"I'm counting on it," Barton answered.

The moment he was gone, I said loudly, "You can come out now."

"What gave you the impression that I was eavesdropping?" Emma asked with a grin as she came out to join me. She was petite, with fine red hair, freckles that sparkled when she blushed, and pale-blue eyes.

"I don't know. Call it a hunch," I answered with a smile of my own. "Emma, you know that you could have asked me for time off yourself."

She frowned a moment before she spoke, and her expression served to remind me just how young my assistant was. "I wanted to, but Barton insisted that *he* do it. Are you sure you don't mind?"

In response, I hugged her. "As long as you come back to Donut Hearts, we're good."

"I promise," she said.

I only hoped that Emma could keep her word. Working with her boyfriend on his dream might prove to be too tempting for her, but she was a grown woman, even though she was barely into her twenties, and that was ultimately a decision she'd have to make for herself.

I decided not to worry about it and go about my business.

After all, I had customers to feed, and now I had a weekend party to get ready to attend. Two weeks would ordinarily be plenty of time for me to get ready for three days away from the donut shop, but this was a different story altogether.

I decided to do what any sane woman would do who was in over her head and out of her element.

I called my mother.

CHAPTER 3

"SUZANNE, THAT GOWN LOOKS ABSOLUTELY stunning on you," Momma said as I modeled a dress she'd chosen from the ReNEWed inventory. Barely five feet tall, my mother was still a force to be reckoned with, and I pitied anyone who took her tiny stature as an indication of the size of her spirit.

"Dot is right. That gown could have been made for you, Suzanne," the proprietor, Gabby Williams, said as she watched from nearby. The owner of the shop was a trim woman in her late fifties who always looked nice, but given her constantly churning inventory, it wouldn't be too difficult for her to pick out the best things she brought in and save them for herself.

"I don't know. It's awfully expensive," I said, though I loved the way the dress made me feel. I hadn't worn anything nearly so frilly since my high school prom, and I was surprised how nice it felt to be out of my usual attire of blue jeans and T-shirts.

"Nonsense. We all know that the price tag is merely a suggested starting point for the negotiation," Momma said.

"Suzanne, are you trying to dicker with me?" Gabby asked with one eyebrow arched in the air as she looked at me.

Before I could respond, my mother said, "You're addressing the wrong customer. She won't be the one buying it, Gabby. This is my treat, so I'll be handling the negotiations myself."

"Momma, I can't let you spend this kind of money on me," I protested weakly. If I'd had to pay for it out of my own pocket, used or not, the dress would have blown our monthly food budget, so how could I justify letting my mother treat me to something so extravagant?

"Nonsense. Consider it a late birthday present, or an early one for next year, if you prefer." I was starting to waver when she added, "Jake is going to absolutely love you in this."

"It's still too much to spend on a dress, no matter how fabulous it is," I said, making one last feeble protest.

"Don't you worry about that. Gabby, may we talk?" Momma asked sweetly. "Suzanne, you can change back into your jeans and T-shirt now."

The shop's owner was clearly gearing up for battle. Haggling over a price with me was one thing, but we all knew that my mother was in the major leagues. Gabby had her work cut out for her if she was going to hold her ground and make a fair profit, but I wasn't about to try to rescue her.

I was getting a fancy new party dress. Well, not new, but new to me. As the two women began to negotiate the price in a whispered conversation, I twirled around once more before I changed to go back to my everyday life. I was starting to really get excited about this party, and I was glad that Elizabeth had invited us.

Besides, I couldn't wait to see my husband in a tuxedo.

It was the day before the party was set to begin. I was busy making sure that we were well supplied with flour, sugar, yeast, and a few dozen other supplies we needed on a regular basis for the next few weeks. I liked to place my orders myself, but it took some time, and once I got back from the three-day weekend, I wouldn't have time to do anything other than make and sell donuts. While it was true that I'd have Emma's mother, Sharon, helping me out in the kitchen, it just wasn't going to be the same. At the moment, Emma was running the front, and I was ensconced in my tiny little office in back, trying to decide how much flour I really needed to get me through until my next order. We were well into the cold-weather months, and folks seemed to like donuts more when it was brisk out. I tried to order based on what I'd needed the year before, but I wasn't cranking out widgets at the donut shop, and things never seemed to stay the same. The fact was that I never knew from day to day, let alone month to month, which of my donuts would outsell the others or how much inventory I needed to create each day. I hated making too few donuts and turning hungry people away, but at the same time, I was loathe to donate or, worse, throw away, too many unwanted treats at the end of the day. It was a perilous way to make a living, but I wasn't complaining. I'd been born to be a donut maker. I just hadn't realized it until I'd bought the place after my divorce from my first husband, Max.

"Suzanne, do you have a second to spare? You have a visitor," Emma said as she poked her head in through the door.

"Is it important?" I asked, distracted by the numbers dancing around in my head. As a small-business owner, I had to wear a great many hats, and the truth was that some of them were more comfortable than others.

"It's one of the ladies from your book club," she said. "She seems a little on edge."

"Is it Elizabeth?" I asked, wondering if my friend was having second thoughts about throwing the elaborate party.

"I'm not sure. Is she the redhead?" Emma countered.

"No, that's Jennifer," I responded.

"Then it's Jennifer," Emma said. "Do you want to come out and speak with her in front, or should I send her back here to you?"

"Ask her to come back to the kitchen," I said. I wasn't sure what Jennifer wanted to discuss with me, but I knew that we'd both be more comfortable chatting out of the public's view.

Jennifer Hastings, the fearless leader of our little book club, came back a minute later, dressed as always in an elegant fashion that put even my best friend, Grace Gauge, to shame. No, that wasn't fair. If Grace had the money at her disposal that Jennifer surely must have had, I was positive that my friend would have dressed just as stylishly.

"So, this is where the magic happens," Jennifer said with the hint of a smile as she looked around. "Funny, but I always pictured your kitchen workspace as being bigger."

"Oh, it is. There's another wing just through there," I said with a smile as I pointed to the back door.

"Really? No, of course there isn't. You're just teasing me," she answered with a smile of her own.

"I'm excited about the party tomorrow," I said. "Is that why you're here?"

"In a way," Jennifer said, and then she glanced down at the papers strewn across my small desk. "I've caught you at a bad time, haven't I?"

"No worries. I'm just catching up on some supply orders, but it's nothing that can't wait for a friend," I said, doing my best not to show any impatience about wanting to get back to it. It was clear that something was bothering her. "Jennifer, is everything all right?"

"I'm not sure," she said with a frown. "Hazel suggested that I come talk to you in person. She would have come as well, but she's dealing with a minor crisis of her own."

"What's wrong?" I asked, wondering what my friend had gotten herself into. The ladies might have had a great deal more money than I had, but their lifestyles clearly didn't come without problems of their own.

"Her cook is threatening to quit again," Jennifer said. "It

happens more often than you might realize. Some of our friends are extremely predatory about other people's staff."

I should have such problems myself. Not really, though. I enjoyed cooking for Jake and me, and I couldn't imagine letting anyone else do it on a regular basis. Well, maybe Momma, but it would be more of a voluntary thing than a paid position. "She's still coming to the party though, right?"

"Oh, she wouldn't miss it. That is, if there's still going to be one."

"Has something happened?" I asked her, concerned that Elizabeth's newly found hope for her marriage had somehow evaporated.

"Yes. No. Perhaps. The truth is that I'm really not sure."

"At least you nailed down all of the possibilities with your answer," I said, standing and moving toward her. This was clearly a conversation that was going to take some time, and I didn't want to have my order forms staring at me as we spoke. "Why don't you tell me what's happening?"

Jennifer sighed heavily, paused for a few moments to collect herself, and then she said, "It might be nothing, but my husband, Thomas, and Jason belong to some of the same groups. For the past several months, Thomas has been hearing rumors about Elizabeth's husband that have him concerned."

"What kind of rumors? Like extramarital affairs?" I asked her, remembering Elizabeth's earlier suspicions.

"Hazel and I have suspected for some time that Elizabeth's husband is a little too close to his personal assistant, but it's not just that," she said. "Evidently Jason's company is in trouble. He came to Thomas about securing a loan last week. When my husband asked to see his books as a matter of course, Jason said there was no real need for him to do that. He said that they had known each other for years, and that he should trust him. If you knew my husband, you'd know that it's not a matter of trust.

He *always* wants to make sure of what he's getting himself into. After all, we're talking about a great deal of money here."

"I understand completely," I said. I knew that these people were all wealthy, clearly well beyond my means, but that didn't mean that they didn't have more serious problems than who was poaching whose chef at any given moment. "It sounds like a reasonable enough request to me. Why would Jason refuse to show your husband his books?"

"That's one of the things that alarms Thomas so much. That led my husband to ask around, and while he didn't learn anything specific, he heard enough to worry him about some of Jason's current business associates. Also, if things are so dire with his firm that he needs a sizable cash infusion to bail out his business, why are he and Elizabeth throwing this lavish party? I understand keeping up appearances, but it doesn't seem prudent to me, given the circumstances."

"What can we do?" I asked. "Should we talk to Elizabeth?"

"That's just it," Jennifer said with a frown. "We can't say anything directly to her, at least not without proof. Elizabeth hasn't been this happy in months, and I for one would hate to be the one who ruined it for her."

"Even if she's heading straight for a train wreck?" I asked.

"Especially then. Think about it, Suzanne. What if Thomas is wrong about Jason and his situation?"

It was time to turn the tables. "You know your husband better than anyone. Is he *usually* mistaken about things like this?"

"Never in my memory," she admitted. "That's not all, though. It gets worse."

"Worse than what you've told me already?"

"You knew that Hazel's husband, Reg, owns a chain of insurance agencies, didn't you?"

"I hadn't heard, no," I admitted. It had never come up during our book club meetings, just as I was fairly certain none of the ladies knew that my husband was a former state police investigator.

"Well, one of his employees told him that Jason recently applied for a great deal of life insurance."

"Maybe he's just trying to protect Elizabeth," I posited. "It could be that he's trying to take care of her if something should happen to him."

"That's the thing. The policy wasn't on him. It was for Elizabeth."

"Now *I'm* worried," I said.

"What should we do?" Jennifer asked, clearly distraught about the situation.

"I'm going to talk to my husband," I replied.

"No disrespect intended, but what can *he* do about it?" Jennifer asked, clearly puzzled by my suggestion.

"You may not be aware of it, but he was the best state police investigator on the force," I said. "If anyone can get to the bottom of it, it's Jake."

After letting out a sigh, Jennifer said, "I feel better knowing that."

I didn't want her to get the impression that he was some kind of miracle worker. "He'll do what he can to help, but I'm not sure he can prevent anything bad from happening," I said.

"I understand that. Just knowing that he's going to be there takes a load off my mind." Jennifer glanced back at my paperwork before she added, "I've kept you long enough. I'll see you tomorrow evening."

"You can count on it," I said.

After she was gone, I stared at my order forms for another minute before finally giving up and calling my husband. I wanted to share what I'd learned with Jake, but I didn't want to do it over the phone. Was Jennifer just being paranoid, or did we all have a reason to fear for Elizabeth's happiness, not to mention her safety? Either way, her husband would bear watching at the party.

Unfortunately, what had begun as a fun and festive event had now turned into an investigation, not of murder but of the *possibility* of something bad happening.

It was one thing to hunt a killer down.

It was quite another to prevent something from occurring before it happened.

But that was exactly what Jake and I were going to have to do if Jennifer's and her husband's hunches turned out to be correct.

"What's wrong?" Jake asked me the second I walked into the cottage we shared after I finished work for the day. I'd shut the donut shop down, run my reports, made my bank deposit, and finally, I'd driven the short distance home to find him sitting on the couch, engrossed in a book. I glanced at the title and saw that it was on poisons, an odd topic for most folks but just standard reading material for him. Though he was officially retired from the force, his mind tended to focus on all things criminal, which might be a good thing, given what I was about to tell him.

"What makes you think something's wrong?" I asked him as I slipped out of my jacket and hung it up by the door.

"Suzanne, I don't need a mood ring to tell me that something is bothering you." Tall and thin, Jake sported a shock of sandy blond hair that was just beginning to thin, a sign that we were all getting older. It wasn't fair, though. While I was starting to look more and more like my great-aunt Louise, Jake seemed to get more handsome with every passing day.

"Jennifer Hastings came by the shop this morning," I said as I plopped heavily down beside him. "She told me some things about Elizabeth Martin and her husband that are troubling."

"You've got my attention," he said as he put a marker in his book and set it to one side. "Go on. Is he seeing his personal assistant again?" I'd shared my suspicions with him when Elizabeth had first come to me, and Jake hadn't forgotten a single detail of our conversation.

"I'm beginning to wonder if he ever stopped," I said, "but that's just the tip of the iceberg. He asked Jennifer's husband for a loan recently, but when Thomas wanted to check his financial records, Jason changed his mind and withdrew the request."

"That could mean a great many things," Jake said reasonably enough.

"Maybe, but that doesn't explain why Jason took out a large life insurance policy on Elizabeth recently."

Jake took that in for a few moments before speaking again. "I admit that that is a bit curious. Did he take one out on himself as well at the same time?"

"I didn't think to ask her that," I admitted.

"Do me a favor. Give her a call and find out."

I shrugged as I pulled out my phone. I was sure Jake had his reasons to make the request, and I wasn't about to question what they might be. Luckily I had Jennifer's number in my phone's memory. "Hey, it's me."

"You're not coming, are you?" Jennifer asked, clearly troubled by the prospect.

"Don't worry. We'll be there. Jake wanted to know if Jason took out a policy on himself when he took the one out on Elizabeth," I said. "Is there any way you can find out?"

"Give me one minute and I'll call you right back," she said, and then she disconnected the call.

"I'm waiting for an answer," I told Jake as I put my phone down. "Jennifer's worried about Elizabeth's situation, and so is Hazel. No matter what we find out about the life insurance, could we dig around a little into Jason's business and his life before we go to the party?"

"Are you talking about starting an investigation today?" Jake asked, clearly surprised by my suggestion.

"Well, next week would probably be a little too late, don't you think?" I asked my husband with a grin.

"Yes, I see your point, Suzanne, but there are questions that need to be asked of people who are under no compulsion to speak with us. It has to all be handled delicately and, if at all possible, under the radar. You realize that, don't you?"

"It's usually the only way I know how to operate. I know it's not going to be easy, but we at least have to try, don't we?" I asked him.

"Of course we do," he said as he patted my hand. "Take it easy and let me make a few calls. Like I said, this needs to be done delicately."

"Are you implying that I'm not subtle?" I asked him with a grin.

"You are many things, my dear lady, but subtle is not one of them."

Jake was just reaching for his telephone when mine rang.

"Hang on a second before you make your first call," I said.

As I suspected, it was Jennifer. "Hazel said the two of them took out policies on each other. Is that significant?"

"I'm not sure. It could be. Thanks."

Jennifer paused a moment before she asked again, "We will see you tomorrow evening, won't we?"

"I wouldn't miss it for the world," I said.

"Excellent. That's great news."

After we hung up, I told Jake, "They took out policies on each other."

"So, there may not be any cause for alarm there after all. If he'd taken out a policy on her life only, it might be suspicious, but it could just mean that they've decided to make sure they are each taken care of if something were to happen to either one of them."

"What about his supposed mistress, his personal assistant? How personal is she? And why wouldn't Jason let Jennifer's husband see his books? Don't forget, he might have some shady ties in business, as well."

"I'm not discounting any of the possibilities," Jake said as he started dialing. "Let me call someone I know who might be able to help without raising concern on anyone else's part."

"Is it a former colleague?" I asked him.

"I suppose in a way you could call him that. Topper's had some useful inside information for me in the past when it came to business connections."

"Are you saying that he's a snitch?" I asked my husband, surprised he'd use someone like that as a resource.

"I think they prefer to be called confidential informants," Jake said with a grin.

"And he's a *friend* of yours?" I asked.

"Suzanne, I have all kinds of acquaintances, but that doesn't necessarily mean that they are friends. After all, in my job, there were only two kinds of people I generally had much contact with; some of them were on one side of the law, and some of them were on the other. If you don't want me calling Topper though, I won't, but I'm warning you, we're not going to be able to dig up a tenth of what he'll be able to tell me off the top of his head, especially given the short notice. It's your call, though."

I thought about it less than five seconds before I nodded. "Call him."

"Are you sure?"

"I'm positive," I said. After all, if Jake trusted this man, then so did I. Besides, he was right. What choice did we really have? I'd grown adept at investigating murder in the past, but this was clearly beyond my scope.

Jake made the call, sounding for all the world as though they were best friends. After he finished, he said, "It shouldn't be long. Now we sit tight and wait."

"It occurs to me that I don't know everything there is to know about you," I said softly.

"Why would you?" he asked with a hint of laughter in his voice. "After all, I had a life before we met, and so did you. Isn't that part of the fun, getting to know each other better every day?"

"I suppose so, but I thought it would be more like finding out your first crush's name, not something like this."

"Her name was Jillian. She was my babysitter, and I remember her being an older, beautiful woman. It turns out that she was only three years older than me at the time."

"Did you also discover that she wasn't very pretty, either?" I asked him.

"Oh, no. She was incredibly attractive. I ended up running into her a few years before you and I met, and if anything, she'd just gotten prettier over the years."

I wasn't sure I was happy with that answer. I knew it didn't make sense to be jealous of this woman from my husband's past, but I couldn't help myself. "Did you two finally go out?"

"No, it was clear that she kind of resented the fact that I was arresting her for attempting to murder her business partner, so I didn't even ask her out," Jake said with a grin.

"My, you've led an interesting life, sir," I said with a returning smile of my own.

"And to think that it's not even over yet," he admitted as his phone rang.

"That was quick," I said as he started to answer it.

"But we still don't know if he found out anything we can use. Let's see if he was able to get anything."

CHAPTER 4

AFTER A FEW MINUTES OF conversation, Jake hung up, frowning.

"What did Topper say?" I finally broke down and asked when he wasn't in any hurry to volunteer the information.

"Evidently Jason Martin took out a sizable loan in the past few months from some pretty shady sources. He's got some large payments due pretty soon, and if he doesn't pay them, he's going to have more problems than he bargained for."

"So maybe there's a reason he took out a large life insurance policy on Elizabeth after all," I said.

"It's certainly something to keep in mind. Suzanne, I know you're not a fan of me going anywhere armed, but I'm starting to believe that I should take a weapon with us tomorrow."

"I was just about to suggest the same thing," I said.

"Really?"

"Really. The truth is that I'd feel better knowing that you were armed. I'm tempted to take my baseball bat I keep under the register myself."

Jake smiled at my suggestion. "I understand the impulse, but it might be a little hard to explain to the other guests. Don't worry. Once we get there, we'll find you a blunt object to use yourself. Are you sure you don't want to take a class and get a weapon of your own?"

"No, thanks," I said. "I'd probably end up shooting myself

instead of the bad guy. No, I'll stick to a baseball bat. At least my weapon can't go off accidentally."

"Neither can mine, if I handle it properly," he said. "Is this going to ruin the party weekend for you, Suzanne? I know you were looking forward to a fun time without any worries or responsibilities."

All I could do was shrug. "It is what it is. It's not going to be the party I was hoping for, but we're needed, Jake. What choice do we have?"

"If I ever needed a friend, I couldn't imagine anyone better than you," he said, and then he offered me a tender kiss.

"You'll never have to worry on that count. I've got your back, Jack," I said with a grin.

"It's Jake, not Jack," he answered, smiling in return. "How quickly they forget."

I had a difficult time getting to sleep that night, and I stopped my alarm a full three minutes before it was set to go off. I had one more morning of making donuts at the shop, and then Jake and I were leaving for the penthouse that Elizabeth and her husband had procured for the weekend.

It would be tough getting through the day, but I didn't have much choice.

The donuts needed to be made, no matter what issues I might have on my plate at the time.

"Hazel, I didn't think I'd see you until tonight," I said as the third member of our book club came in just before closing. She was a plump, older woman, with a normally ready smile that was distinctly absent at the moment. "Is the party still on?"

"Yes, despite my best efforts," she said with a heavy sigh.

As she studied my nearly empty display case, she asked me, "Suzanne, do you have any bear claws? I'm so stressed out all I can think about is food." Hazel was constantly struggling with her diet, and there were times I felt bad about enabling her, but hey, I never said a steady diet of donuts was good for anybody. Every now and then though, a tasty treat could satisfy a sugar craving better than just about anything else.

"Are you sure you want one?" I asked her, despite my earlier pledge not to interfere.

"I'm positive," she said. "Hand it over."

I grabbed the last bear claw, put it on a plate, and slid it across the counter to her. "On second thought, maybe I'd better get that to go," she said.

As I made the bear claw transition from plate to bag, I asked, "What did you say to Elizabeth to try to get her to cancel the party?"

"I tried to tell her that the weather report was so dicey that we should cancel it for everyone's sake, but she said that it was nonsense. She wasn't about to let a little rain or sleet ruin her weekend."

"I thought we might get snow or even freezing rain?" I asked her. It was all my customers had been able to talk about all morning. We were always in an odd position when it came to predicting our weather. There were instances in the past when towns nearby got snow while we got only rain, but sometimes when they got rain, we got the freezing variety, which was the worst of all worlds, in my opinion. Ice accumulated on everything, and even at a quarter of an inch, it could bring power lines and large tree branches down. I loved snow, and there was even room in my heart for rain on a hot summer day, but freezing rain and I did not get along well at all.

"That's what I told her, but she wouldn't listen to me. Is there any chance you'd speak with her yourself, Suzanne?"

I thought about it, but then I shook my head. "I'm sorry, but it doesn't make sense. You and Jennifer have both already tried, and you are her oldest friends. I'm afraid I would be shouting at the wind if I tried it myself."

"I understand," she said. "At least some of the other guests are cancelling."

"Because of the weather?" I asked.

"That's the excuse they are all using, but I have a feeling there's more to it than that."

"How many people were originally invited?" I asked. "And just how big is this penthouse where we'll be staying? I was under the impression that this was going to be a small, intimate party for just the book club and our spouses."

"You didn't know?" Hazel asked. "Apparently it's grown all out of proportion since Jason started adding folks to the guest list, too. I've been told that there will be plenty of room for everyone, even if every last invited guest were to show up. It's the entire penthouse floor of a high-rise apartment building near Charlotte. Elizabeth's husband invested heavily in it. Evidently the problem was that they couldn't rent space on any other floor after they sank all of their money into the project."

"Why not? Is it built that badly, or is it the location?"

Hazel frowned. "From what Reg heard, it's a little bit of both. The contractors took quite a few shortcuts, but there's something much worse, at least in this modern age. The entire place is in a cell phone dead zone. They've been working to get a signal there that doesn't require all kinds of electronic boosters, but so far they haven't had much luck. Even *with* the boosters it's hit and miss, but when the power goes out, which happens quite frequently according to my husband, the place is one big dead zone. Evidently Jason isn't quite the business whiz he thought he was. Anyway, twenty-four people were invited originally, but when I spoke with Elizabeth, she told me that only six other couples would be there now."

"There's Jennifer, me and you, as well as our spouses," I said, counting the book club. "Who else will be there?"

"Jason's assistant is going to be there with another woman from the office, and some mystery man and his wife will be attending, too. Evidently he has something to do with one of Jason's businesses. I asked Elizabeth for more details, but I honestly don't think she knows anything more than that. The last couple have been their friends forever, but Elizabeth seemed to think there was some fresh bad blood between Jason and the husband. This weekend is going to be an absolute nightmare, Suzanne. Isn't there anything we can do?"

"I wish I could come up with something, but the only thing I can think of is to be there for Elizabeth if she needs us," I said.

Hazel took a step closer. "Jennifer told me your husband was a police officer," she said softly, though my only customers were too engrossed in their donuts to bother with our conversation. It wasn't exactly a secret, either. Everyone in town knew what Jake's former occupation had been.

"He worked for the state police, but he's retired," I said.

"Still, it's good to know that he'll be there," Hazel said, "just in case."

"Just in case" of what I wasn't sure, but I simply nodded. "I think so, too." It was almost closing time, so I said, "Hazel, I hate to rush you, but I need to close the shop so I can go home and get ready for the party."

"Of course," she said as she started for the door.

I called out to my remaining customers, "It's closing time, folks, so if there's anything else you'd like, it's time to make your picks."

Once everyone was gone, I'd started to lock the door when Hazel came back, tapping insistently on the door.

"What's wrong? Did you forget something?" I asked her when I opened the door back up.

"I was halfway out of town when I realized that I forgot to

pay you for my treat," she said as she tried to shove a ten-dollar bill at me.

"First of all, that's way too much, and second of all, you don't owe me a thing; it's on the house."

"I can't let you do that," she said, still shoving the money at me.

"Hazel, if you hadn't come in when you did, I would have just donated it to the soup kitchen, so we're good."

"Fine," Hazel said as she stepped past me and shoved the bill into the tip jar on the counter. "There, I didn't pay for my bear claw after all."

I thought about retrieving her money and returning it to her, but I honestly didn't have the energy. "Thanks. I'll see you soon."

"I'm glad you're coming," she said, and then she was finally gone.

"What was that all about?" Emma asked me as she walked out to collect the last of the dirty dishes.

"Have you been eavesdropping on my conversations out here again?" I asked her with a smile.

"Hey, it gets lonely back there. Are you really still going to that party? Dad said the weather was going to be atrocious by nightfall."

To be fair, Emma's father, Ray Blake, often predicted calamitous events in order to sell more newspapers, so the man wasn't exactly the voice of reason and moderation in April Springs.

"We should be there in plenty of time before bad weather hits, so I think we'll risk it anyway," I said as I started running reports in our cash register. "Do you have big plans tonight?"

"I'm helping Barton get ready for his grand opening," she admitted. "It's taking quite a bit more time than we thought it would."

"Are you still going to class?" I asked, chastising myself even as I said it. It wasn't my job to make sure that my coworker was attending college, but then again, Emma was a great deal more to me than just an employee.

"Yes, Mom," she said with a grin. "I have to admit though, I'm stretching myself a little thin at the moment."

"I know it's a lot of pressure on you both, but you'll be fine," I said, doing my best to reassure her, even though I wasn't sure that they'd be okay at all.

"Thanks, and thanks again for the time off," she said as she headed in back to finish the last of the dishes.

"Just be sure to come back to me," I whispered softly under my breath.

"Did you say something?" Emma asked as she turned quickly.

I must have spoken louder than I'd intended to. "No, it was nothing. I was just talking to myself," I said.

"Okay. As long as you don't start answering, you should be fine," she replied, laughing it off.

I was worried about Emma, but at least her situation wasn't pressing.

I had more on my mind at the moment about the party and my friend Elizabeth's state of well-being.

On the two-hour drive to Charlotte, maybe Jake would be able to help settle my vivid imagination.

If not, I was going to be in for a long three days.

"Suzanne, I'm worried about this weather," Jake said as he looked up at the sky from his place in the passenger seat of my Jeep. His truck was parked safely back at the cottage. It was fine in good weather, but sometimes it seemed to get stuck even if there was just a heavy dew, and we were already getting a great deal more than that at the moment. It had been spitting rain for most of the way, but at least for the moment, none of it was freezing on the windshield. In his retirement, my husband had, among other things, become some sort of amateur meteorologist, watching weather trends and recording information from the backyard weather station I'd gotten him for his birthday. The equipment sensed and recorded everything from the wind speed and direction to the rainfall to the high and low temperatures of the day. There were even functions to it that I didn't understand, but Jake did, and that was all that mattered. My idea of weather forecasting was sticking my hand out the window. That told me all that I needed to know about the weather. If it was chilly, I grabbed a jacket. If it was raining, I got my raincoat. And if it was hot, I forgot about a coat altogether.

It was simple but effective.

"It's just rain," I said as the wipers cleaned the slate of glass yet again.

"For now, anyway," he said, frowning at the sky as though it had offended him.

"Aren't you at all worried about tonight?" I asked him.

"I'm reserving judgment at the moment," Jake said stoically. "There's a very good chance that nothing out of the ordinary is going to happen."

"That may be true, but we still have to be ready in case something does," I reminded him.

"You know me. I am ready and able to handle anything that comes my way," Jake said.

"Except the weather," I answered, teasing him slightly.

If he noticed my teasing, he didn't respond. "Wow, this building is really on the outskirts of the city, isn't it?" Not only was that true, but the surrounding land looked to be in tough shape as well. There were several buildings that had been started and then suddenly abandoned, and it gave the area a kind of postapocalypse feel.

"It's not very inviting, is it?" I asked him.

"At least the top floor and the roof are both lit up," Jake said as he pointed skyward.

He was right. The lobby and eleven stories of dark floors sat just below the top lit one, and there was a mass of floodlights perched on the roof itself that lit up the darkening sky. As I recounted the floors once more, I came to a jarring conclusion. "The penthouse is really the thirteenth floor, isn't it?"

"I'm sure they don't call it that."

"Maybe not, but it's the thirteenth all the same."

My husband touched my arm lightly. "Feeling a little superstitious, Suzanne?"

"I've got a host of bad feelings about this weekend. The fact that it's the thirteenth floor is just icing on the cake."

"Or the penthouse on top of the building," Jake said with a shrug. "We don't have to go in, you know. April Springs isn't *that* far away."

"Would you really drive another two hours in bad weather just to miss this party?" I asked him.

"In a heartbeat, weather and all."

"Come on," I said with a grin, forcing myself to be positive. "We'll find a way to have fun."

"That remains to be seen," he replied as we got out of my Jeep and made our way to the front door of the lobby.

There was just one problem, though.

It was locked when we tried to open it, and the entire lobby was dark.

I pulled out my cell phone, forgetting that we were in a dead zone of service, but I couldn't get a signal to call any of my friends.

Maybe we wouldn't be going to the party after all.

CHAPTER 5

"WHAT SHOULD WE DO?" I asked Jake as we stood at the darkened door.

"Is turning around and going home an option?" he asked me gently.

At that moment, I saw someone approaching us with a flashlight in their hands. The stranger was two steps from the door when the entire lobby lit up, showing that it was a security guard.

"Sorry about that," the heavyset man apologized as he unlocked the door and let us in. "Sometimes the motion sensors for the lights in the lobby don't catch on that somebody's there immediately. Are you with the Martin party?"

"We are," I said. "I'm Suzanne Hart, and this is Jake Bishop."

"Come on in and I'll check the list," he said as he stepped aside.

After we were inside, he locked the door solidly behind us, and I could see that it was comprised of solid steel, not the lesser aluminum I'd been expecting to find.

"Is that really necessary?" Jake asked him.

"Sorry, but I've got strict orders to keep the outside door locked at all times." As he moved to the desk, the lights in the lobby flickered for a few moments and then came back on at full strength.

"The motion detectors again?" I asked him.

"No, that was because of the main line. This weather is playing havoc with our power."

"Is this building safe to be in?" I asked him.

"Oh, she may seem a little vulnerable when the lights flicker on and off like that, but she's strong. Don't worry. The entire first floor glass is not only shatterproof, it's bulletproof, too. The locks are state of the art, made from heavy steel, and it would take a man with a blowtorch eight hours to get through them. Once this place is locked down, nobody or nothing short of a stick of dynamite is going to get through," he said. Was that meant to reassure me? It felt as though we were about to be imprisoned in a modern-day cell. "Here you are," he said as he scanned the list, using his heavy finger to mark his speed. "You're the last two to arrive. I'm glad you made it. I'm late for my supper as it is, and if I know my wife, she's already started without me."

"Does that mean that you won't be staying?" I asked him.

"No, my shift ended ten minutes ago. Don't worry, though. You'll be plenty safe upstairs."

As he led us to the elevator, he punched the button, but it didn't light up immediately. The guard had to hit it three more times before it responded to his summons, each strike harder than the last.

"Does it always do that?" Jake asked him, a little concern creeping into his voice.

"Just when the power's acting up," he said nonchalantly.

"I'm not sure I even want to get on this elevator," I told Jake as the doors opened.

"Suit yourself. It's twelve flights of steps up though, and the door locks in the stairwells are a bit finicky. They've got some kind of electronic gizmos on them. If you ask me, I'll take an old-fashioned lock that uses a key any day of the week."

I thought about climbing those stairs with our bags and

finally decided to trust the elevator after all. "Come on, Jake," I said as I stepped inside.

"Are you sure?" he asked me.

"Why not? After all, what's life without a little adventure?" I asked him, trying my best to put on a brave face.

As we got in the elevator, I saw that the guard was already heading for the exit.

It appeared that this party wouldn't be chaperoned, so it was going to be up to all of us to make sure things didn't take a dark turn in the course of the weekend.

"Hello, Suzanne. I'm so glad you could come. You must be Jake?" Elizabeth asked as she met us at the elevator, first smiling at me and then offering her hand to my husband.

"How did you know we were here?" I asked her as she took our coats.

"Benny isn't good for much, but he can at least use the intercom," she said.

"This place is lovely," I said as I looked around. The wide-open entry area had been decorated perfectly, with just the right amount of furniture, rugs, lamps, and art to make it look as though it had been ripped from the pages of a design magazine. The floors were made from some kind of exotic hardwood, and the art hanging from the walls looked as though it was worth more than my donut shop.

"It should be, for what it cost to build and furnish," she said. "If you'll follow me, I'll show you to your suite. We hired a full staff to work the entire weekend, but it seems the possibility of bad weather has kept nearly all of them from coming."

"We'd be happy to pitch in and help," I offered.

"Hopefully it won't come to that, but I appreciate the offer." After Elizabeth led us down a long hallway, I noticed that there were some friendly faces, as well as people I didn't know, standing around a piano as a woman sat there playing rather well. I caught Jennifer and Hazel's gazes for a quick moment each, but they merely nodded and stayed where they were. Neither woman looked particularly at ease, and I had to wonder if Jake and I might have missed something already.

"Is everything all right?" I asked Elizabeth gently.

"It's fine. Just fine," she said, clearly lying to me.

"Elizabeth," I said sternly as Jake pulled a little ahead of us. I wasn't about to let her dismiss my question so cavalierly.

"Later, Suzanne," she said. "Please?"

"Of course," I said, wondering what had already rattled her so much. After we passed the living room space, I noticed a large, formal dining area. I was going to need a map to show me around this place. Elizabeth finally led us into another open space, where a series of doors stood closed along a perpendicular hallway. "This is your suite," she said as she led us into an elegant space that was nicer, and larger, than the entire first floor of our cottage. It, too, had been decorated with only the best furnishings. It came as no surprise to me that I felt instantly out of place in the sophisticated decor. After all, my cottage was filled with old furniture that didn't match, battered old hardwood floors that needed to be sanded, stained, and finished, and a fireplace that could use a good scrubbing. In other words, for Jake and me, it was the perfect cozy space, the antithesis of all of this opulence.

"What do you think?" Elizabeth asked me, obviously proud of the space.

"It's lovely," I replied.

She grinned at me slightly, and I could see my friend's true nature return, if only for an instant. "I don't like it, either. It's all a bit oppressive, isn't it? I prefer French Provincial myself."

To me, that style was just as stuffy as this one was, but I

wasn't about to insult my hostess by saying so. "Really, I think it's great," I said, forcing myself to show some enthusiasm. "How about you, Jake? What do you think?"

"It's fine," he said, spending his words as though they cost him money. I'd been hoping for a little more from him, but I'd take what I could get.

Elizabeth instructed us, "If you'd like to freshen up, feel free to join us in the living room whenever you're ready. Candida is favoring the group with music."

"Is she part of the planned entertainment?" I asked.

"No," Elizabeth said with a frown. "She's one of our guests my husband chose to invite at the last minute."

It was clear that Elizabeth hadn't been consulted about the late additions, or approved of them, either. "Got it. We won't be long," I said. Before she could go though, I grabbed her arm lightly. "We're still going to have that talk a little later, okay?"

"That's fine," Elizabeth said in a faltering voice, and then she left us.

"That was odd," I said once Jake and I were alone.

"She seemed a little distracted, but given the circumstances, it's understandable, don't you think?" he asked.

"I know that throwing a party of this magnitude must take a great deal of focus, but there's more to it than that," I said. "I wonder if her husband has been up to his old tricks again?"

All Jake could manage to do was shrug. "I wouldn't know. We're here, Suzanne, and we'll do what we can to keep things under control, but it's not in our power to save her marriage."

"Maybe not, but we can at least watch her back and make sure she stays safe."

"Really?" he asked me gently. "And how exactly are we going to accomplish that? We can't exactly follow her around like a pair of lost puppies."

"I don't know how we'll manage to protect her, but I'm sure

we'll think of something," I said. "Now let's hang up our party clothes and join the others. The sooner we get started figuring out what is going on here, the better."

"Sorry we didn't come over and say hello when you arrived," Jennifer said softly the second we joined her and Hazel, now positioned several feet away from the piano. They had clearly broken away from the main group, which was still intently listening to the woman who Elizabeth had referred to as Candida playing classical music. She seemed to be lost in her performance, not even noticing our arrival or the other women's absences.

"We didn't mean to be rude," Hazel supplied softly.

"No need to apologize. What's going on with Elizabeth?" I asked, dismissing their regrets. As far as I was concerned, none were needed. After all, we were friends, and that status brought with it a certain latitude in the niceties of normal social interaction.

Before either woman had a chance to reply, Jake said, "I'm just going to have a look around, if you don't mind."

"I'll catch up with you later," I promised him.

Once he was out of earshot, Jennifer said, "Elizabeth won't tell us what's going on. When we first arrived, it was obvious that she'd been crying, but when we pressed her about it, she wouldn't talk about it with either one of us."

"This is bad, Suzanne. We're supposed to have a formal dinner this evening and then dancing afterwards, but I'm not sure anyone is in the mood for a party right now," Hazel said. "Will you try to get her to speak with you about what's going on?"

"I already tried," I admitted, "and I failed miserably, I might add. I'm not sure there's anything we *can* do but go along with the planned schedule, at least for the moment. Once things settle down tomorrow morning, hopefully the three of us can get her off to one side and speak with her. Can you tell me anything about the other guests?"

Jennifer pointed to a dapper man with slicked-back black hair and wearing an elegant suit. He was poised protectively over the woman playing the piano, who was dark and brooding, but that might have just been her normal expression. I would say that she was pretty, in a severe kind of way. "That's Bernard Mallory and his *companion*, Candida," Hazel explained as she stressed the word. When she noticed me studying them again, and then her, she added, "Don't look at me that way, Suzanne. That's how we were introduced. Whether she's his wife, his girlfriend, or his paid escort for the evening, I could not say. Evidently Bernard is the one responsible for most of Jason's loans."

"Does that mean that man over there is Jason's childhood friend?" I asked as I pointed to an overweight man with graying hair. He was accompanied by a thin, rather prim woman with the iciest gaze I'd ever seen in my life.

"Yes, that's Henry Jackson and his wife, Lara," Hilda said softly.

"Wow, she doesn't look happy about being here, does she?" I asked.

"Wait until you speak with her. It's even worse. She's been trying to get her husband to leave since the moment they arrived," Jennifer said.

"Where are the others? I thought there would be more people."

"Our husbands are off talking business," Jennifer said. "They'll be joining us shortly."

"Cheyenne and Joan are still in their rooms," Hazel said. "As I said earlier when we chatted at the donut shop, there were several other invitations sent out, but they all cancelled."

"Was it really because of the weather?" I asked as I watched my husband hover around the edges of the group without really joining in.

"That's the excuse they used, anyway," Jennifer said.

"You mentioned two women still in their rooms. Are they a couple as well?"

"No, Cheyenne is Jason's personal assistant," Jennifer explained. "From what I understand, Joan was invited at the last minute as a way of making it less obvious that Cheyenne is clearly here at Jason's insistence."

"I can't believe Elizabeth is allowing her to be here, especially since she suspects them of having an affair," I said.

"That makes three of us," Hazel said. "Jennifer and I agree with you. Oops, here comes Bernard and his *companion*. I didn't even notice that she'd stopped playing. If you'll excuse me, I need to check on things in the kitchen."

"I'll go with you," Jennifer added.

"Are you both just going to leave me here alone to face them?" I asked my friends with a smile.

"We wouldn't dream of doing that to you. Look, Jake is coming over, too, so you won't be alone. We'll catch up more later, Suzanne. Good luck."

I wasn't sure why she was wishing me luck, but a few moments later, I got it.

Bernard and Candida turned out to be quite a pair.

As Jake joined me, they introduced themselves, and then Bernard looked at me and said, "You must be the famed donut maker I heard our hostess talking about. I've never met someone who made donuts for a living before."

"Well, now you can say that you have," I said, doing my best to smile at what I was certain wasn't a compliment. "I understand you are a business associate of Jason's."

"Our paths have crossed occasionally in the past," he said as breezily as he could muster. "How do you like the penthouse?"

"It's certainly decorated to the nth degree, isn't it?" I said, trying to be polite.

"That was all Candida's doing," Bernard said proudly. "She's quite an interior designer, wouldn't you say?"

"I like nice things," Candida said, her stern expression breaking into a brief grin for a moment.

"That must be interesting, being a professional designer," I said. "You're clearly a woman of many talents."

"Oh, I would never do it for the money. I took this project on as a favor to Bernard." She narrowed her focus to Jake for a moment before speaking next, and I had the feeling she was trying to guess his weight by the way she was measuring him from head to toe. "You must be Jake. What exactly is it that you do?"

"I'm retired," he said simply, not supplying any more information than he had to. When he wanted to be, my husband could be most circumspect.

"You seem awfully young to leave the workforce," she said smoothly. "You must have done very well for yourself while you were gainfully employed."

"Financially? No, not particularly," Jake said bluntly. "I get by, but no one in their right mind would think that I was rich."

At his declaration of limited assets, Candida appeared to lose all interest in my husband, which somehow pleased me. "Oh. That's interesting," she said, though it was obvious she didn't find it particularly fascinating at all. "If you'll excuse us, Bernard, we need to start getting ready for dinner."

Her companion frowned at her for a moment before replying. "You go ahead. I need to have a word with Jason first."

Her capacity for petulance was suddenly on full display. "*Must* you talk business this weekend?"

"It won't take more than a minute," he assured her before turning to us. "If you'll excuse us?"

"Of course," I said.

The moment they were gone, I told Jake, "Wow, she was really interested in you, wasn't she?"

"Right up until the moment she realized that I was broke," Jake answered with a smile. "Look at that."

I glanced in the direction he was subtly gesturing and saw that Bernard and Jason were having a whispered conversation. I couldn't make out their words, but their demeanors were clear enough. They were having a fight about something, even though neither man raised his voice the entire time. When Bernard finally broke away and headed for his suite, Jason looked shaken. "Should we press him now that he's on edge?" I asked Jake.

"It might not be a bad idea at that," he said, but before we could manage to get to him, the other couple present cut us off. Henry and Lara Jackson seemed to have impeccable timing, at least if their aim was to keep us from interrogating Jason Martin.

"You must be the couple we've all been waiting for," the man said. "I'm Henry Jackson, and this is Lara, my wife."

"It's a lovely name. Was it taken from *Dr. Zhivago*? I loved the movie *and* the book when I was a teenager," I said.

"It's from my aunt, actually," she answered sternly. "The truth is that I *despise* that movie because of my name. Now I know there's a book to hate as well."

My oh my, wasn't she a bright bit of sunshine? "Are you and your aunt close?" I asked, trying to salvage at least something from the conversation.

"Not particularly. She's been dead for years," Lara said simply.

Okay, that was strike two.

Jake saved me from striking out yet again by jumping into the conversation, or at the very least, diverting it. "Henry, I understand you and Jason grew up together," he said to the stranger.

"Yes, we were inseparable as kids," the man said wistfully.

"Sometimes the past should be left in the past, though," Lara said sternly. "I still don't know why we are here, after the way he swindled us both."

"I've told you a thousand times, Lara, *everybody* lost money on that deal. We can't blame Jason for things going badly. You keep forgetting that he lost a great deal of money, too," Henry said, clearly tired of repeating the explanation to his wife.

"Don't be such a fool, Henry. Look around you. Does it look like your old buddy lost money on *any* deal he ever made? He played you for a fool, and you've proven that his assessment was true by coming here at all. To make matters worse, you dragged me here with you. Unless he has a check in his hands to replace our life savings you so foolishly squandered, I'm not interested in hearing his apologies."

"Lara, you need to look at it from his point of view," Henry started to say as his wife simply turned and walked off. "She's just a little tired from the trip," Henry said, trying to justify his wife's behavior. "If you'll excuse me, I'll go check on her."

"Of course," I said smoothly.

After they were gone, I started looking around for Jason. It didn't even surprise me to see that he was having an angry conversation with a striking blonde who couldn't have been more than a few years into her twenties. She looked as though she were about to explode and make a real scene, but then Elizabeth suddenly appeared, and things somehow found a way to get dramatically worse. The two of them began shouting at each other, and neither one of them did anything to keep the rest of us from hearing them.

"You don't need to be here, Cheyenne," Elizabeth said loudly. "I want you gone, and I mean now!"

"I was invited by your husband," she said defiantly. "I'm not going anywhere."

"He didn't clear it with me, so as far as I'm concerned, you're not even here," Elizabeth said.

"Dear, I explained it to you earlier. I need her here for some work we need to do later," Jason said, trying to step in between the two angry women. It was a risky move, especially given the state of their tempers. "It just didn't make sense *not* to invite her. There's no reason to be suspicious. After all, Joan is here, too."

"Do you think that helps matters any? She's nothing more than a smokescreen, and we both know it."

"You don't know what you're saying," Jason said, trying to mollify her.

I could have told him it wasn't going to work. "We'll discuss it later," Elizabeth said in a cutting tone. "I have to be sure the staff is ready to serve dinner."

Another woman I assumed was Joan—the other invited employee—took Cheyenne's arm and led her away before anything else happened.

It was quite a warm-up to dinner.

Little did I know that it was just the beginning of what was about to turn into a deadly weekend.

CHAPTER 6

"I F I COULD HAVE YOUR attention," Elizabeth said a few minutes later, "dinner will be served promptly in thirty minutes. We have requested formal attire for the evening, so we will see you all back here then."

With that, we all broke up into groups and headed to our suites.

"That's some crowd your friend has gathered out there," Jake said as he sat on a chair by the bed. "I kept waiting for a fight to break out at any second."

"Don't you think what we've already witnessed could be categorized as fighting?" I asked him as I got undressed. I wanted to take a quick shower before I got into the gown Momma had bought me. "Do you mind if I go first?"

"Be my guest," Jake said. "I might just catch a quick nap while you're showering."

"I know you are normally good about being able to fall asleep quickly, but do you honestly think you can do it right now, given the circumstances?" I asked him, envious about his ability to sleep almost anywhere at will.

"I don't know. Let's see," he said with a grin as he spread out on the bed and shut his eyes.

By the time I got out of my shower, he was fast asleep. I knew that he didn't need much time to get ready even wearing the rented tuxedo, so I waited until I was dressed and started applying my makeup before I woke him.

All it took was me whispering his name. "Jake," I said softly.

He came awake instantly, alert and clearly ready for action. It was fascinating to watch.

"Wow. Suzanne, you look even more beautiful than usual," he said as he gave me a long, low whistle after studying me carefully.

"Thank you, kind sir, but I haven't even put on any makeup yet."

"In my opinion, there is no need to gild the lily," he said with a smile. "I like you better just the way you are."

"I appreciate that, but you've lost your mind if you think I'm going out there without my full makeup on. I've picked up enough tips over the years from Grace to dazzle you. Just you wait and see."

My husband smiled as he embraced me, crinkling my dress a little in the process, but the moment that bothered me was the day I knew that I was in serious trouble. "You should realize by now that you *always* dazzle me, Suzanne."

"I appreciate the sentiment, but hadn't you better start getting ready yourself? You're taking a shower too, aren't you?"

It was clear that he hadn't given it much thought, but after a moment, he nodded and smiled. "Of course I am. How much time do I have?"

I glanced at the clock. "If that's accurate, you have approximately eleven minutes."

"That's fine, but what are we going to do with the seven minutes I'll have left after I shower and change?" The sad part about that was that he wasn't even kidding.

"I'm not sure what you're going to do, but I'm going to need every second I've got to make myself pretty," I said. Before he could reply, I added, "You know what I mean."

"I honestly don't, but do whatever you feel you need to do."

After Jake showered and dressed in his tuxedo, it was my

turn to whistle. "Why, if it isn't James Bond, international man of mystery."

"No, thanks. I'm plenty happy with being plain old Jake Bishop," he said with a grin.

"There's nothing plain about you right now," I said, and then I kissed him soundly.

"I thought you were running short on time," he said, smiling, after we broke it.

"There's always time for a kiss," I told him. "Should we talk about what we've seen so far while I finish getting ready?"

"I thought you had to focus on the task at hand?" Jake asked me.

"I can still chat while I work," I said. "What do you make of our dinner companions?"

"Every last one of them seems as though they are a single match away from becoming a bonfire," he admitted, "with the exception of Jennifer and Hazel. I can't speak for their husbands, since we haven't met them yet. I'll say one thing, though. Elizabeth is wound tighter than a clock spring at the moment, isn't she?"

"Can you honestly blame her?" I asked as I worked on making my eyes look more alluring. Grace could have accomplished it in two minutes, but I was having a devil of a time with the technique she'd shown me a few days before. "Her marriage is shaky, her husband is not only a cad, but he's in trouble financially, and he can't even seem to get along with his oldest and best friend. I still can't believe Jason swindled Henry and Lara out of their life savings. Some friend he must be."

"You need to remember that we have only Lara's word that it was all a con," Jake reminded me.

"Henry didn't contradict her, though, did he?"

"Not out loud, but I doubt that woman would take to being crossed lightly," Jake said. "Still, I think she's the only one in the family holding a grudge."

"Maybe so. What about the others?"

"Bernard Mallory and Candida are a real pair, aren't they? Tell you what. I think it's time that I call in a few favors and see what I can find out about them." As Jake took out his cell phone, he frowned. "I thought they had a signal booster or something here."

"What's wrong?"

"I can't get a single bar on my phone," he said.

"Maybe it has something to do with the storm," I said as I glanced outside. We were high enough, and it was dark enough outside, that I didn't have a clear view of the ground. All I could see was the windowsill and spots of the thinnest ice beginning to accumulate in areas already. "It appears that the rain is starting to freeze."

"It's a good thing that we're safe and inside, then, isn't it?" Jake asked.

"I think so," I said. "So, what do we think about Bernard and Candida in the meantime?"

"He's a little too slick for my taste, if you know what I mean. As for her, sometimes when she speaks, it's as though she's playing a role instead of being herself. I wonder what her real story is? I have a feeling beneath that frosty veneer is nothing more than a frightened little girl."

"Really? I didn't get that at all. The truth is though, it might be worth our while to find out," I said.

"What about Cheyenne? She's pretty blatant about her attachment to Jason, isn't she?" Jake asked, pursing his lips as he considered the administrative assistant.

"They were clearly arguing about something before Elizabeth even approached them," I said. "I thought the two of them were going to come to blows at one point."

"They may yet before the evening is over," Jake said.

"I hope not. I hate seeing Elizabeth this stressed." I studied

Jake for a moment before I added, "This isn't much fun, is it? I'm sorry I dragged you into this."

"You don't have to apologize to me, Suzanne. While it's true that I'm not sure I'd call it a laugh a minute, at least it's not dull," Jake said as he kept fiddling with the cuffs of his shirt under his jacket. "I hate these monkey suits."

"Does it help any that you look spectacular wearing it?" I asked him.

"Maybe a little, but I still can't hold a candle to you. You're the one really shining. If your customers at the donut shop could see you now, they'd forget all about your delicious treats and focus solely on you."

I smiled as I thanked him for the compliment, applied a few more touches to my makeup, and then I put everything down on the mirrored dressing table. "I'm afraid that's the best I can do."

"I want to ask you something, and I'm dead serious," he told me.

"What is it? You know that you can ask me anything." If Jake really wanted to go home before we had a chance to even eat dinner, I wouldn't argue or fight him about it. Elizabeth was my friend, but my husband meant everything to me.

"Would it ruin your makeup if I kissed you again?" Jake asked me.

"I don't know. Let's try it and see," I answered with a grin.

It took a minute to repair the damage that we did, but it was worth every second of it.

"Are you ready for dinner?" I asked Jake.

"I suppose it would be rude not to show up at all, wouldn't it?"

"Besides the fact that we wouldn't have anything to eat, yes, it would be rude," I reminded him.

"You twisted my arm. You know me. I can't stand the thought of not being polite."

"Or missing a meal, either," I said with a smile.

"I won't argue the point. Come on. Let's go."

We walked into the main dining hall, me with my arm in my husband's and feeling like a fairytale princess.

Apparently we were again the last ones to show up, and as everyone stood there waiting for us, I heard a woman scream from the back of the room.

CHAPTER 7

T O MY SURPRISE, IT TURNED out that it was Joan who had screamed, the nondescript employee who had pulled Cheyenne out of the room earlier.

"What is wrong with you?" Cheyenne asked her harshly as she turned to stare at her.

"This," Joan said as she held a cocktail napkin out with a trembling hand toward her coworker, who was quite obviously not a friend, based on her treatment of the woman.

From where I stood, I could read the note before Cheyenne took it from her.

It said, *"DO US ALL A FAVOR AND JUST DIE!"*

"Who would write such a thing to you?" I asked Joan as I stepped forward.

"I can't imagine! I've never hurt anyone in my life! Why would someone say such a horrid thing to me?"

"Are you sure that it was meant for you?" Jake asked her. He'd moved closer to stand beside me, but I hadn't even noticed him step up, I had been so focused on Joan. I wasn't the only one. Jake plucked the note from her fingertips before Cheyenne could secure it for herself. It looked as though she wanted to protest his behavior, but one look at my husband's expression must have told her that it would have been pointless to complain.

"What do you mean?" she asked him, clearly confused by the question. "Who else could it have been meant for?"

"He wants to know exactly where you found it," Jason said firmly. He'd been a few steps away from her himself, but unlike my husband, he'd made no move to acquire the note. "It's a perfectly reasonable question at that. Where *did* you get it, Joan? And what exactly have you been up to?"

"I didn't do anything!" she squealed, getting riled up again after just starting to settle down. After she took a moment to compose herself, she answered Jason's original question. "It was on the bar over there. I found it when I made myself a drink," she said, gesturing to the wet bar in the other room. "I didn't have a coaster, and I was afraid of putting a ring on the table."

I headed straight for the bar, and the moment I got there, I started turning over cocktail napkins at a furious pace to see if there were any companion pieces to it.

None of the rest of them had messages on them.

Had the true intended recipient failed to notice the message and left it for Joan to find, or was someone indeed gunning for the most innocuous person at the party?

At that point in time, I honestly had no idea.

"What exactly is it that you do for Jason?" I asked Joan as I pulled her to one side and did my best to keep her calm.

"I'm the firm's chief accountant," she said. "Actually, the most exciting thing that usually happens during my day is when everything balances out nice and neat."

"If I may ask, why are you here?" Henry Jackson asked her as he stepped nearer himself, with Lara just a few paces behind him. Everyone was dressed elegantly, but this wasn't a party in any way, shape, or form. There was so much tension in the room I could almost taste it in the air.

"She's an invited guest, Henry," his wife said. "Don't be rude."

"It's not rude at all," I said. "I was wondering the exact same thing myself."

Oddly enough, Bernard Mallory and his date, Candida, hadn't seemed at all surprised by the accountant's presence. Was it possible that Joan was there upon their request? If Bernard wanted to get to the bottom of Jason's ability to repay at least the interest on his loan, why *wouldn't* he want an accountant there? I had to wonder if he could trust Joan, though. Shouldn't Bernard have brought an accountant of his own? Or was that another one of Candida's other hobbies?

"I'm not exactly sure why I was invited myself," Joan confessed in a mousy voice. "I got an email two days ago saying that my presence was required here this weekend. That's all that I know. The truth is, I'm as much in the dark as any of you." She sounded as though we'd been browbeating her, which we hadn't, but I'd known some generally passive people in the past who would shut down upon the first hint of an attack, whether it was real or not.

"It's not exactly a mystery as to why you are here," Jason said. "I'm getting ready to do some restructuring within my firm, and I need answers to my questions instantly. Besides, Joan has been a good and loyal worker for me for years. I thought the weekend might be a nice reward for all of her toils on my behalf in the past."

"Some reward that turned out to be," Cheyenne said sarcastically.

"That napkin wasn't meant for *you* by any chance, was it?" I asked her.

The administrative assistant whipped her head around as she stared at me. "Why would you even think something like that, let alone say it?"

"Well, proximity for one thing. You've been beside Joan since you arrived, at least when you haven't been near Jason," I explained.

I hadn't meant it to be biting, but the observation was true enough. Cheyenne had been hovering near her boss since we'd arrived, with the single exception being when Elizabeth was nearby. At least the personal assistant seemed to have *some* kind of survival instinct.

"I always stand nearby in case I'm needed," Cheyenne said formally, not making eye contact with any of us. "It's my job."

"If that's your job, then you do it a little too well for my taste," Elizabeth replied, her voice growing louder as she spoke.

Jennifer and Hazel had both stepped closer to their friend, as though they were trying to protect her in some way. On the other hand, I seemed to be leading the charge, asking embarrassing and uncomfortable questions of everyone, including our host and hostess, if necessary. After all, they couldn't be immune to my interrogation, or the rest would flatly refuse to answer our questions. I didn't know that for a fact, but I was certain of it, nonetheless.

"At least he *needs* me," Cheyenne said pointedly, this time looking directly at my friend.

"Are you implying that he doesn't need *me*?" Elizabeth asked bitingly as she took a bold step toward the woman she suspected of having an affair with her husband.

One step was all she got to take though, as Hazel and Jennifer moved in on either side of her, effectively blocking her forward progress.

The head caterer coughed once at that moment, and then she spoke. "Mrs. Martin, if you're ready, dinner is served." In a near whisper, she added, "My staff has requested that they leave early, due to the storm conditions outside."

That brought everyone's attention to the windows. There

still wasn't much to see there but the darkness that surrounded us. I couldn't even tell if the icy rain was still accumulating outside. There was something isolating about being thirteen stories above the ground, and I wasn't sure I liked it. The two-story cottage I shared with Jake was usually plenty high enough for me. When I'd lived in the bedroom upstairs during the time Momma and I had cohabited after my divorce but before my second marriage to Jake, I'd loved being able to look out onto the park at night, especially in winter. It had allowed me to be close enough to the action but still remain a little above it all.

This was overkill, though.

"I think it stopped," Jennifer's husband, Thomas, finally said. At least I assumed it was her husband, judging by the way she had her arm wrapped in his.

"No, listen closely," the man who must have been Hazel's husband, Reg, replied. "You can hear it tapping against the glass."

"Even so, it's not enough to worry about," Thomas replied.

"Says the man who *isn't* going to be driving home in it tonight," Reg replied, grinning. It appeared the two men were friends as well, given their bantering nature. In a way, it made perfect sense to me. Hazel, Jennifer, and Elizabeth were all so close, and all in the perceived same social network, that it would have been bound to happen that their husbands would at least get along.

"Yes, you're the champion of the common man," Thomas said with a grin.

The caterer shot him a quick glance flush with anger, but she managed to suppress it so quickly that I wasn't even absolutely positive that I hadn't imagined it.

Evidently I hadn't. Thomas saw the look as well, and he quickly apologized. "Please forgive me for being so glib with my friend. We tend to poke each other at every opportunity, and I didn't think before I spoke. I am truly sorry. I didn't mean to be insulting."

"Of course," the caterer said, though her lips were still pressed firmly together after she said it.

Jennifer stepped in at that moment and whispered something quickly to the caterer, who immediately smiled.

"What did I just miss?" Thomas asked his wife, clearly a bit miffed that she'd whispered what she'd said instead of saying it loudly enough for everyone to hear.

"Do you *really* want to know, dear?" Jennifer asked him sweetly, though it was clear there was more than a hint of warning in it. I knew the fiery redhead. If he called her bluff, or what he might perceive was a bluff, she'd tell him exactly what she'd said, and right in front of the rest of us, too.

"Never mind. I said I was sorry. What more can I do?" he asked.

"You can help the caterers after the meal by taking their equipment downstairs to their van," Jennifer suggested.

"I can do that," Thomas agreed happily.

"That's what you get for calling me common," Reg said, chiding the man while he had the chance.

"As a matter of fact, my husband would be delighted to help you as well," Hazel said, giving her spouse a severe look.

"Me? What did I do?" he protested.

She didn't answer, at least not with words. It was amazing to me how much power one arched eyebrow had, though.

"What I meant to say was that I'd be delighted to join you," Reg added quickly.

That got him a kiss on the cheek from his wife, which seemed to be all of the positive reinforcement that he needed.

"Now that that's all settled, let's eat, shall we?" Elizabeth asked. It was clear the entire evening was grating on her nerves, and I suspected that the sooner it was over, the happier she'd be.

"Let's," I said. "But we still need to deal with Joan's note."

"I keep telling you all, it wasn't meant for me!" Joan protested. "And I'd really appreciate it if you'd stop saying that it was."

"The mystery note, then," I corrected. "I don't suppose anyone wants to confess to authoring it, do they?"

What a shock. No one stepped forward.

"Very well," Jake said as he removed an evidence bag from his tux jacket pocket to put the note in. "If you all don't mind, I'll just hold onto this for now." I had been expecting some kind of statement clarifying his position, but it appeared that I was in the minority.

"What are you, some kind of cop or something?" Cheyenne asked him, clearly interested in my husband for the first time that evening. Money might have done it for Candida, but with Cheyenne, it appeared that she was attracted to lawmen. It wasn't that unusual, and it didn't help matters that my husband looked so dashing in his tuxedo, but I still didn't have to like it.

"I used to be, once upon a time," he admitted.

"Interesting," Bernard Mallory murmured as he looked at Candida.

"It can be," Jake agreed.

"I feel so safe just knowing that you're here," Cheyenne said with admiration clear in her voice. I may not have been happy about her giving my husband attention, but Jason was clearly even less pleased.

"You heard the caterer," he snapped. "We won't solve anything this minute, so let's eat before everything gets cold."

As we all walked into the dining room again, I made it a point to put my arm in my husband's. I held him back while the others moved forward so we could have a little chat.

"Surely you're not jealous of her, Suzanne. She's just a child."

"Intellectually? You're probably right about that. But

physically? You're not blind, and neither am I, so don't even bother. She looks all grown up to me."

"Suzanne, don't be crazy. She's young enough to be...." He let the sentence die, but I know that he'd been about to say she could have been his daughter. Jake's first wife had been pregnant when she'd died in a car wreck, and to this day, it hurt him to mention what he'd lost. We'd talked about it ourselves in the past, but it was something he was less and less willing to share with strangers as the years went by.

"Who do you think wrote the note? And was it meant for Joan or someone else?" I asked him, doing my best to distract him from his dark thoughts.

"I honestly don't know," Jake said, "but it bears looking into. In the meantime, be careful. I shouldn't have been so quick to admit that I used to be a cop. Did you see the way everyone closed up when I said it?"

"Everyone except Cheyenne, you mean?" I asked him with a smile.

"This is serious," he replied.

"I know it is. I just don't have a clue about any of it," I answered. "I could see someone leaving it for Jason, but several other folks here could qualify for that kind of harsh message as well. The real question is, what can we do about it at the moment?"

"There's nothing we *can* do," Jake said. "Just watch your step and keep your eyes open."

"I always try to do both of those things," I replied.

"Suzanne, I'm not joking. Someone has a mean streak in them, and it might just escalate into something more than leaving a nasty note."

"I know that just as much as you do," I said. We had to end our conversation as we all returned to the dining room.

"Are you two coming?" Jennifer asked as she noticed that we'd been lagging behind.

"We're on our way," I said, doing my best to put on a brave face.

The truth was that suddenly I didn't feel all that much like a party.

The note, and the revelations that had come afterwards, had put a damper on the atmosphere, and I knew that my husband was right.

It would pay for us both to be on our toes until we were on our way home again.

Whenever that might be.

Maybe Jake had been right after all. His instincts, for whatever reason, had been urging us both back to April Springs.

Only now that probably wasn't an option. With the icy rain still coming down outside, we were all getting closer and closer to being stuck in the penthouse, whether we liked it or not.

CHAPTER 8

A S WE ALL WALKED INTO the dining room, Thomas's cell phone rang. It was a jarring sound, given that we'd basically been in a communication blackout. I wondered if he had some kind of super phone that could pick up a signal anywhere or if the boosters were working again, at least for the moment.

"I didn't think we got reception here," Bernard Mallory protested. Evidently he'd thought the same thing.

"What can I say? A lot of times it's hit and miss," Jason replied.

"Excuse me," Thomas said. "I really have to take this." He looked at his wife for approval, and she nodded.

After a brief conversation, Thomas rejoined us. Instead of addressing his wife, he spoke to Hazel's husband instead. "That was Shag."

"What happened?" Reg asked, the dread heavy in his voice.

"Greta left him an hour ago."

"We need to go," Reg answered, as though it weren't up for debate.

"I know," Thomas said, and then he finally turned to his wife. "Jennifer, he sounds as though he might do something desperate. Is there any chance you and Hazel will leave the party with us?" Before she could answer, he glanced at Elizabeth, not Jason. "I'm sorry to do this, and I wouldn't if it weren't an emergency, but a friend of ours is in serious trouble. Reg and I have known him for years, and if we don't try to help him and something happens to him tonight, we'll never be able to forgive ourselves."

"You can go without me," Jennifer said. "I'll be fine right here."

Thomas clearly didn't like that idea. "Seriously? I hate abandoning you like that."

I was standing close enough to hear her next words, but I doubted that anyone else was. "Elizabeth needs us, too. Go."

"I'll be back first thing tomorrow morning," he said as he kissed his wife.

"Don't take any chances. If the roads are slick, wait until they are salted," she told him.

"If they're icy, I'll skate back," he said with a grin.

Reg looked at Hazel pleadingly. After a split second, she nodded as she said, "Of course you should go with Thomas. Your friend needs you. Besides, the party's going to last for three days. It will be fine. Give Shag my love."

"You are the best," Reg said, and after he gave her a quick kiss, he and Thomas headed for the door.

"What about your bags?" Jason reminded them.

"We'll pick them up in the morning," Reg said.

"How are they going to get out?" Jake asked our host. "The guard downstairs told us this place was some kind of fortress when it's in lockdown mode."

"I'll let them out," Jason said. "I know the code."

"Do you mind if I tag along, too?" Jake offered.

"It's really not necessary," Jason answered, clearly unhappy about my husband's request.

"But I insist," Jake replied calmly. I could have told Jason that he might as well give up. Jake's mind was made up, and he wouldn't change it short of gunpoint. Well, maybe not even then, unless my life was at stake or something equally dire.

"Do you two want to come as well?" Jason asked irritably of

the other men. I was a little offended by not being included, but I knew that the offer hadn't been a sincere one anyway.

"No, thanks. I'm good," Henry Jackson said.

"As am I," Bernard Mallory added.

"Then let's go. The sooner we get you two on your way, the quicker we can eat," Jason said.

"In the meantime, we'll delay our meal a few minutes until you and Jake return," Elizabeth said without much warmth.

That clearly made the caterer unhappy. It was obvious that she wanted to get out of there with her staff before the roads became impassable, and I couldn't say that I blamed her.

I decided that there wouldn't be a better time to get Elizabeth alone than with her husband downstairs with mine. The moment they were gone, I said, "Elizabeth, do you have a second? Jennifer, Hazel, and I would like to speak to you."

"This really isn't a good time," our friend said, clearly not pleased that we were forcing her hand.

"It won't take a second," Jennifer assured her.

"What are we talking about?" Lara Jackson asked as she tried to join us.

"Sorry, but it's official book club business," Hazel said, rebuffing her without remorse.

"Wow, you really take your club seriously, don't you?" she asked us with sarcasm.

"It's important to us," Jennifer said as she took Elizabeth's arm in hers and headed for a quiet corner of the living room. Hazel and I were right behind her.

It was finally time to have that little chat I'd been promised, whether Elizabeth liked it or not.

"What is going on with you?" Jennifer asked Elizabeth the second we were all alone.

"I don't know what you're talking about," Elizabeth protested weakly.

"There's no use trying to deny it, because we all saw it. You were obviously crying earlier," I said.

"Why are you all ganging up on me?" she asked us in a hurt voice. "I thought it was a *good* thing inviting you to this party. This is a chance to celebrate our friendships."

"Are we really *all* friends, though? Six of your guests don't appear to match the rest of us," Hazel said, and then she quickly added, "I'm not being a snob, but I'm not sure why an estranged old friend of your husband and his business partner are here with their significant others, not to mention two women who work for Jason's firm. They don't really seem to fit in under the friendship category."

"I might even understand the rest of them being invited for whatever reason, but I just don't understand why Cheyenne and Joan are here as well," Jennifer added.

"Get in line," Elizabeth said petulantly. She turned to me as she added, "Suzanne, if you must know, *that* was the reason I was crying. Jason sprang it on me at the last second, and we had a huge fight. It was bad enough that he invited that thug and his girlfriend to my party, but to include that tramp? It's insulting to our marriage and the vows we took a long time ago."

"What about Henry and Lara Jackson?" I asked. "Why did he invite them? There's a great deal of anger there, especially with Lara. Henry seems as though he's trying to make it work, but his wife clearly despises your husband."

"Inviting them here was my idea. Henry and Jason have been friends since they were children, and I've hated seeing them fighting this way."

"It's not like this is a childhood spat. They have a reason to be so angry with him," Hazel said before I could figure out how to say it a little more diplomatically.

"What are you talking about?" Elizabeth asked, clearly surprised by Hazel's statement.

"Jason lost their life savings," I said.

"Oh, that?" she asked, trying to brush it off. "*Everyone* lost money on that deal. Besides, Jason didn't make Henry do anything he didn't want to do. Is it my husband's fault that Lara doesn't understand that? I swear, if she'd just realize that in business, not every deal makes money, this wouldn't be such an issue. Even Henry seems to understand, but there's no getting through to Lara. She needs to grow up, if you ask me. You shouldn't gamble if you're that afraid of losing. I know my husband has his faults, but he would never purposely hurt a friend like that."

Elizabeth was defending Jason to the end, even with their problems, and I had to admire that, even though I thought some of her loyalty was misplaced. I loved Jake dearly, but that didn't mean that I had to defend every last one of his thoughts and actions. Besides, she was being a little too cavalier about someone else's life savings in my opinion. It didn't surprise me that I could relate to Henry and Lara more than I could my book club friends. It had been my experience that the only people who said that money didn't matter were the ones who had plenty of it to spare.

"The problem with that attitude is that the Jacksons believe that Jason didn't lose *anything*," Hazel said.

"I'm willing to bet that Lara said that," Elizabeth said with a frown. "She's resented my husband's friendship with her husband for years. That investment was just the latest in a long line of complaints she's had against him."

"Then why is she even here?" I asked.

"Who knows? Jason was flabbergasted when he learned that they'd agreed to attend. I'm willing to bet that Henry is as desperate to save his friendship with Jason as Lara is to destroy it."

"That explains them, but why are Bernard and Candida here? Is that even a real name, Candida?"

"In this day and age, who knows?" Elizabeth asked. "Their presence is odd, I'll grant you that. They just showed up, at least as far as I was concerned, but clearly Jason had invited them earlier. I told him that he was ruining our celebration, and he started yelling at me! He told me that if he couldn't work things out this weekend with Bernard, there wouldn't be any cause to celebrate." Elizabeth bit her lower lip for a moment before she added softly, "Apparently Jason has gotten himself into some kind of financial trouble. I suppose we both are, truth be told, deeper than I've ever seen it in the past."

"This has happened before?" Jennifer asked, clearly surprised by the news.

"It's not something I like to talk about," she said.

"Elizabeth, what it all boils down to is that we're worried about you," Hazel said, which was true enough.

I was certain that Hazel was referring to her emotional state of being, but I had more immediate concerns than that. "Answer one thing for me. Do you feel safe here?" I asked her.

"Of course I do. Suzanne, this building can withstand just about anything short of a direct assault," Elizabeth said.

"That's not what I meant," I said. It was as delicate a way as I could put it, asking her if she was at all worried about the huge life insurance policy her husband had recently taken out on her. Given the state of their finances and their marriage, my inquiry was justified, at least as far as I was concerned. Apparently she was going to make me say it out loud. "I'm talking about the life insurance policy."

"Jason would never lay a finger on me," Elizabeth said, clearly upset that I'd even brought it up. "How did you even hear about that?" She looked at Hazel then and scowled. "You've been talking, haven't you?"

"Suzanne is right," Jennifer said, stepping in. "We've been worried about your safety lately."

"This conversation is ridiculous, and I'm disappointed in all of you for even considering the possibility."

As Elizabeth walked over to the window and looked out, I took some time to think about where things stood now. Was she right? Were we stirring up trouble where there was none? Should I just drop it and assume that everything was going to be all right? I couldn't just let it go, though. Evidently Jason needed serious money, and it appeared that the *only* way he was going to get it would be with Elizabeth's demise. Then another thought occurred to me. What if Jason wasn't the one who had wicked plans for her? If it was the only way for Bernard Mallory to get his investment back, might he do something to expedite his repayment? Then again, it might not even be about the money. What if one of the Jacksons wanted to hurt Jason by eliminating the one person in the world who had his back, no matter what? Then again, could Cheyenne have her own plans for Elizabeth's murder? If she thought that my friend was the only thing standing between her and happiness with Jason, she might do something to accelerate matters. I was getting more worried about Elizabeth's safety than ever before, and then I realized something else. Could that note have been meant for *her* instead of Joan?

Evidently I was lost in my dark thoughts a little too long. When I looked up, I saw that all three women were suddenly looking at me with more than a little curiosity.

"Suzanne, are you okay?" Jennifer asked me softly.

"Sorry, I spaced out there for a few seconds," I said, trying to make light of the dark possibilities I'd just been considering.

"It's more than that, and we know it," Hazel said.

Did I really want to get into all of that right now? I wasn't sure that I was ready to admit any of my thoughts openly without having more proof. After all, I knew better than anyone that my imagination had a way of taking some twisted turns on occasion.

Elizabeth would probably be fine.

The key word was probably.

Still, I had to wonder if I should say something.

I never got the chance, though. I had taken too long to make up my mind.

The elevator door opened, and a moment later, Jason and Jake stepped out together. They'd clearly been discussing something unpleasant, because neither man looked particularly happy with the other at the moment.

I'd lost my opportunity to say something to Elizabeth.

Or had I? Maybe I could get a single warning in while I still had the time.

"Just be careful, okay?" I asked her as I whispered into her ear.

Elizabeth looked at me quizzically, but before she could reply, the caterer stepped forward. She'd clearly been waiting for the men to return, so before any more delays could occur, she announced, "Dinner is now served."

And that was the end of that.

As we went into the dining room together, one phrase kept repeating itself in my mind.

"DO US ALL A FAVOR AND JUST DIE!"

I just hoped that it hadn't been directed at Elizabeth, and what was more, I didn't want *anyone* to try to make the suggestion a reality.

A little later, after the entrees had been served and we were all eating, Lara said out of the blue, "I'm just curious about something, Jason. Exactly how much did all of this cost?"

Elizabeth looked at her oddly before she replied. "I'm not sure I know why you are asking that, Lara."

"It's fairly clear, isn't it? She wants to know why you can afford to throw parties like this if you lost so much money on your investments recently," Bernard Mallory replied, clearly enjoying the woman's audacity to ask such a bold and pointed question in the middle of what was supposed to be a formal dinner party. In my experience, in polite circles, money wasn't usually talked about, but I wasn't sure how polite this particular circle was, anyway. Bernard continued, "It's a fair question that I've been pondering myself."

"You know the answer to that better than anyone, Bernard. Since I'm part of the group that owns this building, there wasn't a fee for using it this weekend," Jason said, clearly unhappy about having to justify his spending habits to his party guests.

"Even so, this food couldn't have been cheap, or hiring the catering staff to prepare it and serve it," Lara said angrily. "Come on, prime rib? Really? Who exactly are you trying to impress, Jason?"

"This was meant to be a celebration of our marriage," Elizabeth said, clearly confused by the direction the dinner conversation had taken.

"That might have been the original intent, but clearly that's all changed," Henry said with a sigh.

"You should answer the woman's question, Jason," Bernard insisted.

"I don't care about all of this," she said as she gestured at our food. "What I honestly want to know is what really happened to our money?" Lara asked as she looked at her husband for approval. I wasn't sure she got it, though. The poor man looked absolutely miserable being in the middle between his wife and his best friend.

Jason looked exasperated by the turn things had taken. "Lara, we've gone over all of this a dozen times before. The investment looked good initially, but there were unexpected contingencies that we had no way of knowing about beforehand. We couldn't foresee any of it, and *every* investor lost money on the deal, including me. I'm sorry, but I never made any guarantees."

"You said it was a sure thing," Lara protested.

"I said it was as close as there was to one that I'd seen in a long time, and I meant it at the time," Jason said. "You need to keep in mind that you're not the *only* ones who got hurt on the deal."

"I can attest to that," Bernard said with a stern look.

"Look, Cheyenne and Joan can show you *exactly* what happened," Jason said. "Plus, they can both testify to the fact that I lost more than anyone else did."

"And yet here we are, eating like royalty in a penthouse," Lara said before taking an angry bite.

"Not *every* deal I've made has lost money," Jason said. "Must we really discuss this at the dinner table?"

"I suppose not," Henry said, caving in. "Lara, let it go. Please? For my sake."

His wife was having none of that, though. Ignoring her husband, she stared down her host as she said, "This isn't over, Jason."

"Can we please just enjoy the food, everyone?" Elizabeth asked, pleading with them to stop.

"Maybe if you'd stop trying to kill the conversation, we could," Cheyenne said softly.

I heard her say it, and clearly, so did Elizabeth.

"That's all I'm going to take from you. Get out!" Elizabeth said angrily as she started to stand.

"Make me!" Cheyenne replied, standing as well to face her adversary.

"Elizabeth!" I said sharply as I stood as well. "May I have a word with you?"

"What is it, Suzanne?" she asked angrily as she looked at me.

"Take a deep breath," I said softly after I'd approached her, "before you say something you might regret later."

"The *only* thing I regret is the guest list to this party," she said.

Was that directed at me? "Sorry. I was just trying to help."

"I appreciate the sentiment, but I don't need your help or anyone else's. I'm a grown woman, and I can handle my life just fine without interference from anyone else." With that, she stormed out of the room.

I started after her, hoping to apologize. What I'd said and done had been out of love and caring, but clearly she hadn't seen it that way.

"You'd better let us handle it," Jennifer said as she patted my shoulder.

"Don't worry. She'll cool down in a bit. Just give her a little time," Hazel added, and the two women went after our friend, leaving me out completely.

I looked at Jake in bewilderment about what had just happened. He just shrugged in my direction as he looked as sympathetic as he could.

"All of this arguing has given me a headache," Lara said suddenly as she stood, too. "I'm going to go to my room and rest."

"Are you going to be okay?" Henry asked her.

"That remains to be seen, but I doubt it," Lara answered. After taking three steps toward their suite, she stopped and looked back at him. "Aren't you coming?"

Henry looked down at his unfinished food, and then he sighed loudly. "Yes, dear," he said.

"Henry, hang back one second," Jason said, but all his old friend would do was wave off the invitation.

"I'm sorry, Jason. I've got to go," he replied as he trailed off after his wife.

After they were gone, Cheyenne asked her boss, "Jason, are

you going to let that woman continue to treat me as though I'm trash that needs to be taken out?"

"She's my wife, Cheyenne. What can I do?"

"You could grow a backbone, for starters," Cheyenne said as she stood as well. "You know what? I'm sick of this."

As she stormed off, Jason asked his other employee, "Joan, would you go with her and make sure she's okay?"

It was fairly obvious that Joan had no interest at all in doing anything of the sort, but it was also just as clear that it had been an order from her boss and not a request. "Sure." She managed another bite of prime rib before she got up, and I was a little surprised that she didn't take her plate with her the way she was looking at all of her uneaten food.

"Well, I must say, you certainly know how to clear a table," Candida said as she looked around the nearly empty dining room.

"Said the barista with delusions of grandeur," Jason snapped in an offhand manner. He obviously regretted his statement instantly. When I looked over at Candida and then at Bernard, I saw them both react with a level of emotion that I hadn't witnessed from them before. Without a word, they both got up and left the table.

It was now down to Jason, Jake, and me, with the caterers still looking on. I had eaten a fair amount of food, but suddenly I'd lost my appetite, given the tension in the penthouse, and I was guessing that Jake felt the same way.

"How did this go so badly so quickly?" Jason asked aloud, more to himself than to either one of us.

"Excuse me, sir, but will they be coming back?" the caterer asked anxiously. "We really must be going soon."

"At this point I don't even care. Let them all starve! Clear it all away," Jason said as he stood and threw his napkin on the table. "Nobody deserves a dinner this nice."

He didn't even glance at us as he headed toward his own suite.

Now it was just the two of us.

I pushed my plate away, and Jake did the same.

"Sir? Ma'am?" the caterer asked us. "Are you finished?"

"We are," Jake said as he stood. "Let us help you. After all, your original two volunteers already took off."

"We'll be fine," she said as she clapped her hands twice, and the rest of her crew suddenly appeared. It was obvious that they'd been waiting for the signal, because the dirty dishes were emptied and placed in bins on carts almost immediately. Their speed was amazing, and in no time at all, they were ready to leave.

The only problem was that they couldn't.

"I hate to disturb Mr. Martin, but we need someone to let us out of the building," the caterer said apologetically.

"We don't need him. I can do it myself," Jake said.

"I'll go with you, too," I said.

"There's no reason you have to do that, Suzanne," he said. "I won't be a minute."

I looked around the empty room. "What else do I have to do here? Elizabeth's not talking to me, Jennifer and Hazel are consoling her, and everyone else is mad at each other."

"Don't worry. It'll be okay," Jake said as he patted my shoulder.

"If you don't mind, we'd really like to go now," the caterer interrupted. "I'm afraid the weather is going to get worse before it gets better, and we have families we want to be with," she explained.

"Then by all means, let's get you on your way," Jake said.

I had a sudden thought. "Do you need to get paid first? Is that why you need to see Jason?"

She grinned at me for a moment before she answered. "No,

that's already been taken care of. We *always* collect our fees before the meal."

"That's smart of you," I said as I followed them into the elevator. "Are you sure there's enough room for me, too?" I asked as I looked at the crowded space.

"We're not leaving you here alone, Suzanne. We'll scoot in closer," Jake insisted.

I almost turned down the ride. After all, I knew I was being childish, hurt from Elizabeth's rebuff, but the truth was I didn't want to be in that penthouse without Jake, even if it were only for a few minutes, as he'd promised.

"Thanks," I said as I got on.

"The more the merrier, I say," the caterer added just as the doors closed.

CHAPTER 9

BECAUSE OF THE CATERERS AND their bulky carts, Jake and I had to stand close together, which wasn't a hardship for me under any circumstances. He knew that I was still stinging from Elizabeth's rebuff, and he reached out and took my hand in his, giving it a gentle squeeze as he did. The sweet and tender gesture was worth more to me at that moment than a dozen roses and a box of chocolates.

Once the elevator doors opened on the ground floor, Jake and I stepped out of the way so the caterers could get out. As promised, the front door was locked even from the inside, and Jake had to enter a special code to get it to open.

"Thanks for coming down with us," the head caterer said. "We've got it from here."

"Let us at least hold the front door open for you," I said.

After Jake took the door, we watched as they rolled their carts out into the parking lot, slipping a little as they made their way, and I was suddenly jealous of their ability to leave.

"Jake, let's not stay," I said impulsively as I watched one of the carts start to go off in its own direction. I'd moved outside with my husband, and the pavement, once wet, was now getting slick with a thin film of ice. Before too long, the roads would be impassable, but we had my Jeep, and I was positive that I could get us home, or at the very least, away from all of the awful vibes in the penthouse above us.

"Do you really want to make a run for it?" Jake asked me, staring intently into my eyes. "What about your friends?"

"It's clear they are all going to be fine without me," I said, letting a little of my hurt feelings creep into my voice.

"Okay, if you're up for it, then you know that I'm game, too," he said as he started to let the door close.

"Wait!" I called out. "Hold it for one second."

He barely managed to catch the door before it could close. "What's the matter? Did you change your mind already?"

"What about our clothes?" I asked. "We're not exactly dressed for travel."

"I don't know. I think I look spiffy," he said as he pretended to dust off a lapel of his tuxedo with his free hand. "And you are stunning."

"I appreciate the compliment, but I'm not sure I want to drive all the way home in this dress. Besides, I need to at least say good-bye to Elizabeth and the girls."

"What happened to us being here to watch out for her? Are you really okay with letting it go?" Jake asked me as we waved good-bye to the caterers. They didn't seem to have any trouble so far, but I could understand the boss's desire to get her crew on their way before things got worse.

"You heard her. Elizabeth was right. She's a grown woman, and I'm not sure I could protect her even if I tried," I admitted.

"Is any of that your pride speaking?" he asked me as we got back on the elevator to go say our farewells.

"Maybe some of it is," I admitted, "but you have to admit that the environment up there is really toxic. Everybody seems to hate everyone else, and I can't stand the thought of being cooped up with those people one second longer than I have to."

"I get that completely," Jake said as he hit the button for the penthouse. "I just don't want you to do something that you might regret later."

"I can't live my life worrying about that," I said. "I'll tell them I had a donut emergency, and we had to go back to April Springs at the last second."

"What kind of emergency is a *donut* emergency?" Jake asked me with a grin. He looked dashing. My husband should wear tuxes more often.

"I don't know. There could be lots of things."

"Name three," he said, still smiling.

I was about to try when all of a sudden the elevator jarred to a halt and the lights all went out, plunging us both into darkness.

It appeared that, at least for the moment, we were trapped.

CHAPTER 10

AS THE EMERGENCY BACKUP LIGHTS flickered on, I asked Jake, "What's going on?"

"It's okay, Suzanne. I've been wondering if we'd lose power tonight." His voice was level and calm, but then again, my husband was used to working under pressure. That was probably the only thing keeping me from panicking at the moment. If I'd been riding the elevator alone, it would have been an entirely different story altogether.

"What should we do?" I asked, looking frantically around the enclosed space for something, anything, that would make me feel better about the situation.

"I think we should give it a few minutes. Chances are good that the power will come back on its own if we just wait it out."

"Shouldn't we at least try to call someone in the meantime to let them know that we're trapped in here?" I asked as I pressed the communication button on the panel and leaned toward the speaker. "Hello? Is anyone there? We're trapped in the elevator!" A hint of panic crept into my voice despite my husband's calming presence.

He reached out and took my hand again, pulling it gently away from the button. "Suzanne, I checked the system out earlier when I was downstairs with Jason. Unfortunately, the other end of that system goes to the front desk, and we both know that nobody's there."

"How long are we going to be trapped in here?" I asked him,

the panic starting to grow in my voice despite my best efforts not to let it show.

"Take it easy, Suzanne. You need to remember one thing; we're not trapped. If we have to, there are ways to get out of this elevator, even with the power off," he replied. "Right now all we need to do is wait."

"But I don't want to be here," I told him a little petulantly.

"That's why we're leaving, remember?" he asked, trying his best to be reassuring.

"I don't just mean this building, Jake; I'm talking about the elevator."

"You're not suddenly claustrophobic, are you?" he asked me. "I've never seen any signs of it before."

"No, not particularly, but that still doesn't mean that I need to enjoy this experience. Could you please show a *little* emotion?" His peaceful demeanor was starting to wear on me a little.

"What do you want me to do, throw myself at the door?" he asked with the hint of a laugh in his voice. "Would that help?"

"You never know until you try. It just might," I said with a smile, trying to mimic his calm.

"Just take a deep breath. We'll be out of here in no time."

I did as he suggested, but it didn't seem to help.

After ten minutes, a time span that felt more like ten hours, Jake was ready to admit that the power wasn't going to come on again anytime soon. "Okay, it's time for Plan B," Jake said.

"Do we actually *have* a Plan B?" I asked him. "Should we bang on the doors and try to get someone's attention?"

"No one would hear us, and besides, even if they could, what could they do?"

"I don't know. You're the one with the plan," I said.

Jake released my hand, and I felt its absence in mine immediately. I knew that it was ridiculous to expect him to get us out of the situation one-handed, but that didn't mean I didn't miss his touch. "Let me try something." Jake moved to the doors and placed his palms side by side, one on each panel. With a mighty heave, he started to pry them apart, but the going was slow. Once I saw what he was doing, I pitched in and started to jam my fingers into the small opening to get a better grip.

"Suzanne, don't!" he yelled, a sound that echoed in the tight space.

I pulled away instantly. "Jake, this is no time to be macho. I can help."

"I'm all for that. I just don't want you smashing your fingers. Pry from the front of the door, not the gap."

That made sense. "Want to try that again? You take that side, and I'll work on this one."

He nodded and grinned. "See? You have a plan, too."

His positive attitude was tough to ignore, but I'd smile once we were outside of the little steel box we were trapped in.

"On three," I said. "One, two, three."

I pushed my palms against my door while Jake did the same on his. Slowly but surely, we managed to force them open enough to allow one of us to squeeze through.

The only problem was that we were between floors at the moment. There was a substantial opening above our heads and another, much smaller one at our feet.

It was clear that we were going to have a difficult time getting out either way, but we had to at least try.

Anything would be better than staying where we were.

At least that's what I thought at the time.

"Crawl through while I hold the door open, Suzanne."

I looked at my husband to see if he was joking or to gauge whether he'd lost his mind. "In this? I don't think so."

"We can always get you another dress if you wreck that one. I'm sure your mother will understand," he said with a hint of ire in his voice.

I wasn't sure of that all, even given the circumstances, but that wasn't what I'd meant. "Jake, I couldn't do it even if I tried. The space at the bottom is too small, and I can't boost myself up to the next floor. You're going to have to do it yourself."

"Okay, I get that," Jake said. "Can you hold the doors open without my help? It should be easier now that they are apart."

"I'll manage," I said. "Can I put my hands between them now, or do I have to keep my palms on the fronts of them?"

"You can hold them any way that works for you," he said. "Go on and try it. I'm not going to let go until you are sure that you can hold them."

"If you keep holding your side open, how will we know?" I asked him. The question was logical enough, at least in my mind.

"Okay. You're right. I'm going to let go. Are you ready?"

I braced myself as I moved my right hand onto his door and kept my left on the one I'd been securing. I was surprised by how much tension was still on the doors, even with the power outage, but it wasn't anything I couldn't handle if I focused all of my strength and energy on the job. "I've got it."

"Are you sure? These things are the latest in elevator doors, at least according to Jason. They work on some kind of hydraulics."

"You can lecture me about their construction later," I said, starting to feel some of the strain in my hands, arms, and shoulders. Was it from the door pressure, or was my imagination playing tricks on me yet again? "Can you boost yourself up there without any help from me? I'm kind of busy at the moment."

"I shouldn't have a problem," my husband said, and I suspected that he was right. Jake had left the force some time ago, but he still worked at keeping himself in shape. He took off his tux jacket and folded it before putting it on the floor. "Are you ready?"

"Yes," I said, trying not to let the strain I was feeling come through in my voice.

"Suzanne?" he asked me softly. Of course he'd be able to tell. "Are you okay?"

"Just do it, Jake," I said, snapping a little in spite of my promise to myself not to let him see me strain with the pressure.

"I'm on it," he said, realizing the situation offered no time to delay.

As Jake tried to step between me and the doors so he could climb out, I could see two things wrong with our plan immediately. There was no room for him, and the doors weren't open wide enough.

I was going to have to take a step back, something that was going to make my job three times as hard as it already was, and I was going to have to push harder.

"Suzanne, I hate to say it..."

"Then don't. I can do this," I said through gritted teeth. Mustering my strength, I willed myself to push the doors farther apart first. They budged a little at first, and then a little bit more, until I was sure Jake could get through.

Then I took a deep breath and stepped as far back as I could manage it. "Hurry," I said as I felt the strain coursing through my entire body. Every ounce of my being was quivering with fatigue, and it was getting worse by the second.

Jake looked at me for a split second as though he was about to say something, but there must have been something on my face telling him not to. Making it look almost too easy, Jake put his palms on the floor and leapt, driving upward and kicking his body through in an instant.

He had just managed to pull himself completely through the opening when I knew that I'd reached my limit.

I couldn't hold the doors one second longer, and they slammed shut as I lost my grip.

I was alone, and based on how my arms felt, there was no way I was ever getting out of there now.

"Suzanne? Are you all right?" I heard Jake call out from above me on the other side of the doors.

"I'm okay," I said, though I was most decidedly not. It was one thing being trapped in the elevator with my husband. His mere presence had given me a calm self-assurance that everything was going to be all right.

But he wasn't there with me now.

After a moment, he admitted, "I can't pry the doors open from here. You're going to have to do it, at least a little bit, so I can get my hands in."

"I'm sorry. I can't," I said as I leaned my back against the elevator and tried to catch my breath. I was already feeling a little better, but I was a long way from being able to do as he'd asked.

I must not have said it loud enough for him to hear me, though.

"What was that? Suzanne, don't quit on me now. What did you just say?"

"I said that I'll try," I answered. I just couldn't bring myself to tell my husband that I was quitting. Rubbing my hands together to loosen them up, I put one palm on each door and put every ounce of energy into pushing them to the sides.

It was a thousand times harder opening them both myself, and I felt my grip slip a few times, but I couldn't let my husband down.

At the very end, just when I thought I was going to fail, the doors finally started to budge a little. The moment there was the least amount of flickering light coming from the other side, a pair of strong hands reached down and pulled them apart.

Our problems were far from over, though.

I had to somehow manage to climb out while Jake held the door, and I honestly didn't think I'd be able to do it.

"Do you have a new plan now?" I asked him lightheartedly as I felt my arms go weak.

"I'll take it from here," Jake said, his voice brimming with confidence. I don't know how he did it, but he somehow managed to force the doors open even more.

"Suzanne, I need you to hold them open again for a second." I could tell by his voice that he hated asking me to do it.

"Even if I could, I can't hold them open and climb out, too."

"You won't have to," he said. "Do you trust me?"

"You know I do," I said.

"Then hold them open."

I did as he asked, and after a moment, Jake wedged something into the opening toward the top.

"What is that?" I asked him as I let go, not waiting for his order.

"I found a fire ax in a case in the hallway," he replied. "Now give me your hands."

"I can't climb, Jake. I'm too tired," I said.

"I'll pull you up. Come on. You can do this."

I wasn't at all sure that I could, but I wasn't going to stop now. After grabbing his tux jacket and handing it through, I couldn't put it off any longer. Reaching up, I gave my husband my hands, and the next thing I knew, I was lying in the hallway beside him just as the ax slipped and clattered to the floor. The doors slammed shut, and I realized that I'd come close to being injured by the elevator doors, even when there was no power going to them. What genius had designed them to be so unwieldy when there was no electricity going to them?

I quickly forgot the question though, mainly because I didn't know who to ask, and at that point, I was honestly too tired to care.

It didn't matter. I was free of at least one of my prisons at last, and I had my husband by my side again.

For the moment, that was all that counted.

CHAPTER 11

"**S**UZANNE, ARE YOU OKAY?" JAKE asked as he helped me stand.

"I'm fine, but I'm afraid I might have ruined my dress," I said. It had torn in a few places upon my release, and there were several smudges of grease along the front of it that I suspected would never come out.

He laughed and hugged me, not caring about anything else but my well-being. "I'll buy you a dozen more when we get out of here. Let's go."

"Are we going back upstairs?" I asked him, not sure my trembling legs could make the journey.

"No. We're much closer to the bottom than we are to the top. You can tell your friend what happened later, but we're not going to risk getting trapped here again. We need to get out of this building right now. Are you okay with that?"

I'm not ashamed to admit that I didn't even hesitate. "Yes, sir. That sounds like a great plan to me."

"Good. Then let's go."

We walked the three flights down and finally reached the lobby. A few emergency lights were on, but the entire area had a weird vibe to it, and I wanted nothing more than to escape this building that was clearly trying to kill me. I knew the thought was irrational, but it was the way I felt nonetheless.

Soon enough though, it was clear that we weren't going anywhere.

"It won't open," Jake said as he tried the door for the dozenth time. "How can they design an electronic lock that won't open in a power outage?"

"Can we break out?" I asked, looking around for something we could use as a battering ram.

"The glass is shatterproof and bulletproof, remember?" Jake reminded me.

"There has to be some way to bypass the lock," I said.

"I'm sure there is, but I don't know how to do it. Jason didn't cover that earlier."

I looked outside and saw that we weren't the only ones without power. The entire area was dark, with the exception of a few flickering lights off in the distance. Apparently some folks were relying on candlepower, but we didn't have a single thing to help us. Then I remembered that I had a flashlight app on my phone. I couldn't afford to drain the battery needlessly, nor did I need any supplementary illumination at the moment, but it was nice to know that I had it in case of an emergency.

As if this wasn't emergency enough.

"What are we going to do?" I asked Jake.

"There's only one thing we can do. You wait here. I'm going back upstairs and find out from Jason how to get us out of here."

"You're not going alone," I said firmly.

"Suzanne, you're exhausted. Don't worry about me. I won't be long."

"No, sir. It's not happening. Besides, I'm starting to get my strength back," I said as I followed him to the stairwell despite his protests. "Whither thou goest and all of that."

"You don't have to do this, you know," Jake said softly.

"I know I don't have to. I want to," I said, and it was true. I would rather trudge up thirteen flights of stairs and back down again than stay there in that lobby alone. "Come on. I'll race you to the top," I said with a grin, trying to make light of the situation and my weariness. The truth was that I really was feeling better. I'd used a good amount of energy escaping from the elevator, but my strength was starting to come back.

He laughed at my challenge, and the sound of it buoyed my spirits even more. It was odd, but by the time we got to the top floor, I was feeling much better. I wasn't sure if I'd just bounced back or if I was on an adrenaline high, but I wasn't going to question it. I took a few moments to catch my breath before we went into the penthouse, but in no time at all, I felt completely like my old self again.

It was time to find out how to get out and then make our escape once and for all.

"Where have you two been?" Jennifer asked us as we walked in. "We've been worried sick about you both."

"We got trapped in the elevator on the way back up," I said.

"Oh, dear. You ruined your dress," Hazel said sympathetically.

"I know. Climbing out of a trapped elevator and crawling across the floor will do that. It doesn't matter."

"It most certainly does," said Elizabeth, who had been holding back in the shadows. The place was so dark that I couldn't really see who was there and who wasn't, and I'd missed her presence entirely. They'd all changed into more comfortable clothing while we'd been gone, and I was going to do that myself at the first opportunity. Party dresses were fine for parties, but this had become an issue of expediency now, and there was no way I wanted to drive home in heels and a ruined dress.

"Jake, let's go change," I suggested.

"In a second," he said as he looked around the room. "Where's Jason?" he asked. "Does anyone know where he is?" The other two couples were present, though the two employees were nowhere to be found. The two pairs hadn't joined us when we'd come in. Bernard and Candida were keeping to themselves by the bank of windows that looked out over a mostly dark area, while Henry and Lara were on one of the couches, whispering like a pair of co-conspirators trying to avoid an indictment.

"He's probably still sulking in our suite," Elizabeth said. "Why do you ask?"

"We need the bypass procedure to get out," Jake said.

"You're leaving?" Elizabeth asked, clearly unhappy with his announcement.

"We want to get out of here before the roads get too bad," I explained. "I'm surprised *everyone* doesn't want to go. It's going to get chilly in here with no power, and there's no telling how long it's going to be off. We'll be right back. We just want to change first."

After Jake and I changed and quickly packed our bags, we rejoined the others.

"We want to leave, too," Henry and Lara said the moment we emerged from our suite back into the living room.

"We are, as well," Bernard added.

"I can't say that I blame any of you," Elizabeth said with a weakened voice. "You all have my blessing to leave."

"Did someone say something about leaving?" Cheyenne asked as she and Joan came out of their suite. They both had their bags. "We were just thinking the same thing. This is no place to be trapped in a power outage."

"We can't go anywhere without Jason," Jake explained. "He's the only one who knows how to open the door when the power is out."

"I'll go get him," Elizabeth said as she started toward the suites in the dim light.

"We'll go with you," Jennifer volunteered.

"It's not necessary," Elizabeth answered.

"Nonsense. We insist," Hazel said, and then she turned to me. "Aren't you coming, Suzanne?"

I wasn't about to say no to that invitation. It was nice to be included in the group again. "I'm right behind you."

"Very well, then. Let's all go." Elizabeth led us to their suite, and I noticed even in the dim light that this was much nicer than our accommodations, as luxurious as they were. Why did it not surprise me that Jason had reserved the best set of rooms for himself?

"What a surprise. He's napping while the rest of us are in a panicked state of emergency," she said with disdain as she pointed to the bed. "Jason. Jason! Wake up! Everyone is leaving." He didn't move, so Elizabeth walked over to the bed and shook his shoulder. "Jason!" Then her voice quivered a bit as she asked, "Does anyone have a light?"

I pulled out my cell phone, happy that for once, I had a strong battery in an emergency. I hit the proper button, and it lit up the corner of the room where Elizabeth was standing over her husband.

The first thing I noticed was her hand. It had quite a bit of blood on it, and it only took a second to confirm where it had come from.

Someone had taken advantage of Jason Martin while he'd been sleeping, and they'd struck him with something heavy from above while he'd been vulnerable.

I raced forward to check for a pulse, but it only took the touch of his skin to realize that he had been dead for some time.

The body was still warm to the touch, but there was not a single sign of life in him.

Our host was dead, and what was worse, until the power came back on, we were all going to be trapped in the middle of the crime scene with no way to get out.

And so was his killer.

I was about to go grab Jake when the other women realized what had just happened. In a split second, Hazel screamed, Elizabeth fainted, and Jennifer just managed to catch her before she tumbled to the floor.

I wanted to stop and comfort my friends, but I had to get my husband in there, and fast. On my way out the door, I couldn't help myself from stopping in front of Hazel and grabbing her shoulders, giving them a firm shake to get her attention. "Hazel. Hazel!"

I knew in the movies that they often slapped people who were being hysterical, but I wasn't about to hit my friend. Fortunately I didn't have to.

"Is he…dead?" she asked me softly as she finally stopped screaming.

"Yes, I'm afraid so," I whispered to her. "I know this is horrific, but you need to collect yourself right now. Elizabeth needs you." I had a feeling that invoking a friend in distress would make an impact on her, and I was relieved to see that it worked. I could almost see Hazel coming to terms with what we'd all seen as she gathered her composure.

"I'll be okay now. Thank you, Suzanne."

"It was nothing," I said as I headed for the door.

"How can you be so calm?" she asked me as Jake came rushing in, no doubt summoned by her very screams.

"I don't know. In situations like this, somebody has to be," I said with a shrug. The truth was that I was pretty good in an emergency. After it was over, I might fall apart, but I could be counted on when it mattered, and that was good enough for me.

"I heard someone scream. What is it? What's wrong?" Jake asked. I noticed that though I hadn't seen a holster while he'd been wearing his tux, and I hadn't even seen it when he'd removed his jacket and leapt out of the elevator, he now had a small handgun out. That's when I realized that he must have used his ankle holster, not that it mattered. I suddenly felt reassured that my husband was armed. As a general rule, I wasn't fond of guns, but my husband was a trained specialist. In his hands, it was a tool like any other craftsman might use in their profession.

"Someone murdered Jason," I said as I pointed to the bed.

That brought a new, soft wail from Elizabeth as Jake rushed over and checked for a pulse, discreetly putting his weapon away as he did.

"He's gone. I already checked," I said, but I knew that he had to confirm the fact for himself.

After a minute, Jake came back over to me. "Suzanne, you might want to get them out of here as quickly as you can."

"Can we at least wash Elizabeth's hands first?" I asked softly. They were both still bloody from where she'd touched her late husband's shoulder and then clasped them together in a state of shock.

"Okay, but you need to do it in the other room," Jake said. "This is a crime scene, and I need to secure it."

"Jake, how are we going to get out of here now? Jason was the only one who knew how to open the door without the power on."

"We can't worry about that right now," he said. "Get them out, Suzanne."

I knew that tone of voice. There was no room for debate. "Ladies, let's get Elizabeth out of here," I said.

Elizabeth had somehow managed to pull herself together, but I noticed that she kept glancing back at her husband's body as she stood there. It was almost as though she needed constant assurance that he was gone and this wasn't just some kind of nightmare. "Is he really dead?"

"I'm so very sorry," I said. "Jennifer. Hazel. I need your help."

That was all it took. Jennifer, forever in charge of us during the book club, stepped up immediately. "Come on, Elizabeth. Let's get you cleaned up."

A sudden thought presented itself. I didn't want to do it, but there was something that needed to be done before I could allow that. "I need to get a picture," I said as I pulled out my phone.

"Can't that wait until we're out of the room?" Jennifer asked.

"We need a record of Elizabeth's hands before we clean her up," I said.

"You need to tell your husband that this is completely out of line," Jennifer said. "This poor woman just lost her husband."

It would have been easy to lay the blame at Jake's feet, but the thought never even crossed my mind. "If you want to be angry with someone, be angry with me. You never know. It might just help protect Elizabeth later." It was true, though it was equally valid that a single photo might end up condemning her. I took the photos despite their protests, much to Hazel and Jennifer's unhappiness. Elizabeth didn't even seem to notice what I was doing, but I was certain she'd be angry about it later as well. I'd mend fences after this mess was all over, but in the meantime, I needed to help my husband solve a man's murder. No matter how unlikable he might have been, he still deserved at least that.

"Who would do such a thing?" Elizabeth asked us all, her voice filled with despair as she let them lead her out of the room. Once again, I was left on the outside of the group looking in, and I wondered if this would be the end of our little book club, no matter what the outcome of our investigation might bring.

My only question at the moment was, out of all of the attendees of tonight's party, who *didn't* have a motive?

Jason was clearly a man with many enemies, and unfortunately, it appeared that one of them had finally caught up with him.

CHAPTER 12

"**I** TOOK SOME PHOTOS OF ELIZABETH's hands before she could get cleaned up, just in case we need to see them later," I told Jake as soon as the women were gone.

"That's good work, Suzanne. I was hoping you'd think of doing that."

"Why didn't you suggest it if it already occurred to you?" I asked him, trying not to stare at the body on the bed. It was difficult not to. As in life, Jason had found a way in death to be the center of attention, good or bad.

This time it was definitely bad.

"I didn't want to interfere with you and your friendships with those women," he admitted.

"That doesn't matter right now. Jake, I need you to think like a cop, not a party guest. Now, what's our first order of business?"

"The first thing we need to do is lock this door," he said. It had a thumb lock on the inside, so at least he could secure it while we were inside. The outside might be another matter, but we'd worry about that later.

"What did they use to kill him?" I asked as I lit up as much of the room as I could with my phone.

Jake did the same, and in a few moments, he found something on the floor near the foot of the bed. Grabbing a washcloth from the bathroom, he returned and picked up a dull cut stone the size of a softball sporting a dull and irregular exterior. The inside was a different story altogether. It had a colorful purple interior that sported a series of sharply defined points, making a hollow opening inside that reflected light from a thousand different facets. Two sides of the stone had been cut smooth in a neat ninety-degree angle.

"What is this thing?" he asked.

"I've seen them before. It's half of a bookend," I said as I started toward the matching piece, still on the bookcase where the killer must have found its deadly twin.

"Don't touch that!" Jake snapped.

"I wasn't going to, but why shouldn't I? It wasn't the murder weapon."

"No, but the killer may have touched it before he got the one he ended up using. Suzanne, you were right before. We have to treat this like a crime scene."

"It's going to be hard to learn anything without a forensics team," I said.

"You'd be surprised. Even today, more cases are solved by good detective skills than a dozen crime labs." I knew that it was a matter of pride with my husband. Jake believed there was a place for science, but nothing could substitute for a keen eye and a sharp mind.

"I believe you," I said as someone started knocking on the suite's door. "What should I do? I shouldn't let them in, should I?"

"No," Jake admitted as he looked quickly around the room. "We're going to have to leave this for now and interview our suspects. Otherwise they aren't going to give us a moment's peace."

"*We?*" I asked him a little incredulously. "You're the pro, re-member? I still have my amateur status, in case you've forgotten."

"Suzanne, I'd take your interviewing skills over some of the partners I've had in the past any day. You have a way of getting people to open up to you that still surprises me."

"It doesn't hurt that your talent pool for assistance is a little limited at the moment either, does it?" I asked him, grinning to show that I wasn't offended by the fact.

"That might be true, but I stand by my statement. You've got chops."

The knocking was now a full-fledged pounding.

"I suppose we'd better answer that before they break the door down," I said.

"I don't guess we have much choice," Jake replied.

I started for the door, but then he stopped me by putting a hand on my shoulder. "Why don't you let me do that?"

"Be my guest," I said.

Truth be told, I was only too happy to let him answer it.

"What?" Jake asked as he opened the door. Henry Jackson was in mid-pound and almost fell to the floor when the door was pulled away.

"Is it true? Is Jason really dead? I can't believe it! I need to see it for myself!"

"I'm sorry, but this is an active crime scene," Jake explained. "No one gets in."

"Why shouldn't I get to see my friend? *She's* not a cop," he said as he gestured to me. "As a matter of fact, neither are you. You told us earlier yourself that you're retired. I have as much right to see him as you do. More, even. After all, the man was my friend for a great many years."

"Just not lately though, right?" I asked him.

"That's a low blow," he said unhappily as he looked at me. "Lara was the one with a problem with him, not me."

"So, are you saying that you don't *mind* that he wiped out your life savings?" I asked him pointedly. There was no time for being delicate.

"Of course I minded, but there wasn't anything he could do about it. That's what I've been telling Lara since it happened. Now let me in."

"I'm afraid that's not going to happen," Jake said in a way that left no room for debate. "We'll be out in a few minutes. Tell the others to stay right where they are. I don't want anyone leaving the penthouse."

"That won't be too hard, will it?" Henry said with a frown. "After all, this is the only floor between here and the ground level with any walls at all."

"What?" Jake asked. "I assumed every floor of this building was outfitted just like this one."

Henry shook his head and smiled sadly. "That's exactly what Jason wanted everyone to believe, but Lara got curious before we came upstairs, and she peeked in the second floor. Then the third. Then the fourth. And so on. They are all just empty spaces. It's a sham. Jason just wanted to make people *think* that the building was completed."

"Interesting. Do me a favor and let everyone know that we'll be out soon," Jake said as he closed the door in Henry's face.

The man looked too stunned to do anything about it, not that he could have even if he'd wanted to. Jake was bigger, stronger, and quite a bit more determined.

"Is that true what he said about the other floors?" Jake asked me once the door was closed.

"I don't know. They are all closed off at the stairwell, and I've been with you the entire time, remember? But the truth is, it wouldn't surprise me. From what I've heard about Jason, it sounds as though it's exactly what he'd do to appear prosperous. At least there's no place for the killer to hide."

"Except in plain sight, you mean," Jake said. "It's obviously one of us. The question is, which one?"

"You can start by eliminating my book club," I said defensively without really giving it much thought.

"Suzanne, I know they are your friends, but Elizabeth *has* to be at the top of our list."

"Granted she had her reasons and we have to at least consider her, but surely you don't suspect Hazel or Jennifer."

Jake was silent for longer than I would have liked, and when he finally did respond, it wasn't what I wanted to hear. "Suzanne, if they thought that their friend's life was threatened, we both know that either one of them might kill Jason to protect Elizabeth."

"They wouldn't do it, though!" I protested. "They didn't!"

"But they *could* have, and that's all we have to go on," Jake answered calmly.

I took a deep breath, let it out slowly, and then I said, "Okay. You're right. Everyone's on the list. Not us, though," I said with a grim smile.

"No, not us. Are you ready to go out there and tackle the room?"

"It's got to beat being here," I said as I glanced over at Jason's body one last time. I'd seen my share of corpses in the past, but it didn't make it any easier, and as much as I'd disliked the man in life, I didn't think he deserved the end he'd gotten. "Let's go."

"After you," he said.

After I stepped into the hallway, I was surprised to see that Jake wasn't on my heels after all. "Are you coming?" I asked him as he hesitated at the door.

"One second," he said, running his hand along the top of the molding of the doorframe. He smiled for a moment as he pulled a shiny, thick wire with a bend in it from the top edge, and I recognized it as a key for newer interior door-locks. As keys went, it wasn't very impressive.

As Jake locked the door and then tried the handle, I asked him, "Is that really going to keep anyone out?"

"Only the honest ones," he admitted, "but it's still better than nothing."

"Do you want me to go around and collect the other keys? I could use a stepladder."

"No, I'll do it myself. While I'm collecting keys, why don't you go in and let everyone know that I'll be right with them?"

"What exactly am I supposed to tell them?" I protested.

"If it were me, I'd say as little as possible," he answered with the hint of a grin. I knew that Jake was unhappy about the murder, but there was also a part of him ready and waiting to leap into action. Investigating crime was too much a part of him to ever let go.

While Jake made his rounds collecting keys, I walked into the living room where everyone was milling about, chattering about what had just happened to one of our hosts.

I knew that this wasn't going to be any fun, but it had to be done.

"What's going on, Suzanne?" Jennifer asked me the second I walked into the room. I'd been expecting to be attacked as soon as I came in, just not by one of my friends.

"All I can tell you is that Jake is looking into what happened," I said calmly.

"We *know* what happened. It's no secret," Elizabeth said. "Someone murdered my husband."

"Believe me, he's trying to be sensitive to that fact, but we still need to conduct an investigation," I explained.

"Why? *He* may be qualified, but we all know that *you* certainly aren't," Elizabeth reminded me, as if I needed the nudge. I was all too aware of my lack of real qualifications, but to be fair, I *had* seen my share of success in the past. I wasn't about to justify my involvement, though. It appeared that Elizabeth was starting to realize that just because we were friends, it didn't necessarily mean that I'd show her any favoritism in our investigation, and she clearly wasn't very happy about it.

"I'm certain that your husband is more than qualified," Bernard said, making it clear that he was not sure of any such thing at all. "But honestly, why should he bother? When the power comes back on, we can summon the real police and be done with it."

"I *am* the real police," Jake said as he walked into the room.

"You said that you were retired," Lara reminded him.

"That may be true, but I still hold reserve state police inspector status for life," Jake said matter-of-factly. "Just because I'm not actively on the force doesn't mean that I don't have all of the powers of an active-duty law enforcement officer."

That was news to me, but then again, Jake kept a great deal about his past professional life to himself.

"Be that as it may, that still doesn't cover *her*," Lara said as she pointed a finger at me.

"I'm pretty sure we all know that you're talking about me without needing any visual clarification," I answered with a wry smile.

Jake shook his head. "As a matter of fact, this time it covers my wife, too. I have the right to designate a deputy under certain extenuating circumstances, and I am officially naming Suzanne as such right now."

Wow, I'd never been a deputy before. "Cool," I said without meaning to say it out loud. It may not have been the best response I could have made, but it was indeed neat that my husband had officially named me as his assistant.

"I don't choose to acknowledge either one of you as having authority over me. I believe that we should wait for the *active* police to arrive," Cheyenne said bluntly. She was forcing Jake's hand, and I wasn't sure how my husband would react to it. One thing was certain; I knew that he wouldn't back down.

Jake didn't disappoint me, either. "Fine. If you'll follow me, please."

"Where are we going?" Cheyenne asked him.

"Anyone, and I mean anyone, who refuses to answer questions will be sequestered until reinforcements arrive."

"What exactly does that mean?" Bernard Mallory asked as he took a step forward.

"I'm locking her up in one of the suites until I have more backup on the scene," Jake explained.

"I'm going with her, if that's the case," Joan said. I hadn't thought they were friends, but evidently Joan felt a little more loyalty to her coworker than Cheyenne clearly felt toward her.

Jake turned and studied the accountant carefully for three seconds before he answered. "No. I'm sorry, but I'm afraid that's not going to happen." It was short and sweet, and it left no room for debate.

Joan appeared to consider pushing him a bit, but after studying my husband's dour expression for a second, she clearly decided that it wasn't an issue she wished to pursue. It was a smart decision, since Jake was clearly in no mood to argue with anyone.

Instead, she turned to Cheyenne and said, "Why don't you just do what he says? There's really no reason to make such a fuss."

Candida surprised us all by saying, "She doesn't have to, and neither do any of the rest of us. I don't know about you, but I don't think he has any right to bully us like this."

Bernard clearly didn't care for his companion speaking up. "Candida, we need to cooperate with the authorities. Fully. Do you understand?" The last bit was said in a chilling voice. Was the man actually threatening her in front of all of us? I wanted to say something, but what was there I could say?

"I'm sorry," she said softly, her resolve instantly broken. Whether her apology was directed toward Jake or Bernard I didn't know, but it was clear that Candida would be cooperating from here on out, and just as obvious who the true bully was. What kind of hold did Bernard have over the former barista?

"Fine, I give in. I'll cooperate! How are we going to do this?" Cheyenne asked. Her eyes were red, and I had to guess that she'd been crying. Was it over her lost boyfriend or the life that she may have created in a fantasy about them living happily ever after once Elizabeth was out of the way? Surprisingly, it appeared that Joan had been crying as well. I had to wonder what had driven her to tears. Had she been that close to her former employer, or was it simply a reaction to a sudden and violent death? I knew from firsthand experience that murder up close could be a shattering experience to endure.

Jake took in a deep breath, and then he let it out slowly before answering Cheyenne's question. "I'm going to take each of you into my suite, one by one. When we are there, we are going to have a brief conversation about what happened, and after we're finished, you are going to come back in here. Now listen carefully, because this is very important. You will not discuss anything with each other before or after I speak with you, and Suzanne is going to be here to make sure you obey that request. Is that understood?"

There were a few noted "yeses" and even more nods. Apparently everyone had decided to cooperate after Cheyenne had been censured.

At least that's what I thought.

Before Jake could call his first interview subject though, Henry spoke up softly. "She made a good point, you know, and you never really addressed it."

"What point might that be?" Jake asked.

I knew the answer, and I had a hunch that Jake did, too, but he was going to make the man say it out loud.

"We should wait for the *active* police, for want of a better term," he said reluctantly. "My friend deserves at least that much."

"And what happens if someone *else* dies while we're standing around waiting for the power to come back on and the local authorities to show up?" Jake asked him. "Do you want that blood on your hands, Henry? Do any of you? Because I can tell you for sure that I for one certainly do not."

"What makes you think whoever killed Jason is going to strike again?" Lara asked with a hint of hesitation in her voice. Her icy demeanor was beginning to show a few cracks around the edges, and I had to believe that the woman was truly frightened. Then again, why wouldn't she be? As far as I was concerned, it was the only sane reaction to have at the moment.

"There could be a dozen reasons," Jake stated, "but I don't feel like going over them one by one with each of you. Suffice it to say that none of us is safe until we figure out who the real killer is." Jake looked around the room for a moment before he asked my friend, "Elizabeth, would you please come with me?"

She looked absolutely shocked when he called her name, but I'd been expecting it myself. If I hadn't known anyone involved, I would have started with her as well. The surviving spouse is *always* the first person to be interviewed in a case of homicide. After all, they usually had the most to gain, and the greatest motive as well.

"You want to speak with *me*?" she asked, clearly incredulous at the impertinence of his request.

"Don't worry. It shouldn't take long," Jake said, trying his best to reassure her.

"It's all right, Elizabeth. I'm going in with you," Jennifer said.

"I am, too," Hazel chimed in.

Jake took a deep breath before turning to look at them each in turn. "I'm afraid that's where you are both wrong, ladies. Just because you are friends with my wife doesn't mean that you get any special favors in this investigation."

"It's okay, Elizabeth," I said, doing my best to reassure her that my husband would treat the matter delicately. "Jake's a good guy."

"No offense, but I'm not sure that I can trust your opinion anymore, Suzanne," Elizabeth said sourly.

There was a real sting to her words, almost like a slap. It had been my experience in the past that whenever someone said "no offense," that's exactly what they meant to do, offend you. After a moment, she turned back to my husband and said, "Let's just get this over with."

Jake shrugged in my direction, offering me his apologies for stirring things up, and then led her out of the room.

I immediately walked over to Jennifer and Hazel and said, "I'm truly sorry about this, ladies."

Hazel frowned as she answered, "Suzanne, we're not supposed to talk among ourselves while your husband is out of the room, remember?"

In a way, she had a point. I couldn't give myself special privileges, not when my friends were being grilled about their possible involvement in murder. I might be free to discuss the case with any of them I chose to, but it wasn't fair for me to try to mend fences while everyone else had been cautioned not to speak.

I just shrugged and walked back to one side of the room. At that moment, I couldn't trust myself to speak. It was pretty clear how my friends felt about my role in this investigation, but there was nothing I could do about that. I had to follow Jake's instructions, and that was all that mattered.

Joan walked over to me a minute later and whispered, "Your friends aren't being very nice to you, are they?"

"They're just under a lot of stress," I said, making apologies for them, even though they had hurt my feelings.

"That's sweet of you to say, but friends don't do that to friends," she said.

"We really shouldn't be talking unless it's about the case," I reminded her.

"That's what I wanted to talk to you about. Is there really any reason your husband even needs to speak with me? After all, I barely knew Jason."

"Apparently you knew him well enough to call him Jason, at any rate," I said.

"Everyone at work calls…called him that," Joan explained. "I never should have accepted his invitation in the first place. He really didn't need me here, at least not professionally."

"Are you saying that you were here because of a *personal* matter?" I asked, zeroing in on her words and what they might mean.

"No, it's nothing like that," she said, flushing a bit as she did. "It's just that…"

"I thought we weren't supposed to talk to each other," Lara said as she looked pointedly at me.

"I'm helping with the investigation, remember?" I asked. "We all just want the same thing, after all."

"What's that, to make it out of here alive?" Candida asked timidly. One look from Bernard was enough to keep her from commenting further.

It was a long six minutes, but Jake eventually led Elizabeth back into the room. "Mr. Mallory, come with me, please."

The only sign Bernard showed that the summons surprised

him was a quickly raised eyebrow that was soon lowered again. "Of course," he said.

Jake gave me an inquisitive look, and in response, all I could do was shrug. I didn't know anything that I hadn't known before, and the odds of getting anything out of this group were growing less and less by the minute. This was one of the most challenging investigations I'd ever been a part of, and our isolation from civilization didn't help matters any.

In a very real way, we were on our own little island, and no one could escape.

Then again, maybe that was a good thing.

The killer, whether they liked it or not, was just as trapped by the storm as we all were.

CHAPTER 13

A s Bernard followed Jake stoically into the other room, I decided to take advantage of the situation and go speak directly with Candida while I had the chance to get her full attention and, more importantly, chat with her away from the one person who seemed to have the most influence on her.

"What do you want with me, Suzanne?" Candida said before I could get within three feet of her. "We aren't supposed to be talking."

"You heard my husband. We're working together on solving Jason's murder, so you should feel free to chat with me," I said.

"Well, I certainly didn't kill him. I had no reason to, for goodness' sake," she protested, her voice devolving into a whine. "What possible motive could I have had?"

"Maybe he made a pass at you, and you lashed out in anger," I said. I was grasping at straws, and we both knew it. After all, Candida had made a good point. Assuming that she didn't have any immediate provocation, what motive could she possibly have? It was pretty obvious that she was somehow under the influence of her companion for the weekend, whether it was a good relationship or not, but I doubted that her willingness to please him included committing murder just because he asked her to.

"He wouldn't dare lay a finger on me," Candida said forcefully, and I could see that she utterly believed it.

"What made you exempt from his attention?" I asked. "He apparently went after just about everyone else."

"That's easy. He wouldn't dare cross Bernard," she explained.

"Why wouldn't he do that?" I asked.

Candida said defiantly, "Because Bernard owned Jason. He was so far in debt that he was *never* going to get his head above water. All it would take would be one word from my boyfriend, and Jason's world would come tumbling down in an instant."

"You might not have a motive, but you just gave Bernard one," I said.

"Really? Think about it. Now that Jason is dead, how is Bernard going to possibly recoup his losses? They didn't exactly have a legal and binding contract. If Jason had a broken arm or leg, then you might be able to justify accusing Bernard, but with the man dead, he's just out of luck."

"He could always go after the widow," I said, remembering the life insurance policies the married couple had taken out on each other so recently. Was murder considered an accidental death in it? If so, I had a feeling that Elizabeth was about to be a wealthy woman, whether she realized it yet or not.

"On what grounds could he go after her? It would call too much attention to him and his operation, and if there's anything he hates, it's the limelight. I hate to be the one to tell you this, but you and your husband are looking at the wrong people as suspects. With the amount of money Jason owed Bernard, it would have been in his best interests to keep the man alive for a very long time."

"You make a good point, but I have a question for you. Do you happen to have an alibi for the time of the murder?" I asked her. She may have been a barista in a past life, but this woman was sharp, and I was starting to see her appeal to Bernard, her physical assets notwithstanding.

"That depends. When exactly do you believe it happened?" she asked me.

It was a fair question, and what was more, it was one I didn't have an immediate answer for. I started thinking out loud. "Answer me this. When was the last time anyone saw Jason alive?"

"Do you mean besides the murderer?" she asked me with one eyebrow arched. The young woman had a wicked sense of humor, which was ordinarily something I liked, but I felt it was out of place at the moment, given the circumstances.

"Yes, of course, besides the killer," I amended.

"I don't know about anyone else, but the last time *I* saw him was just after you two left with the caterers."

I glanced at my watch and saw that it had been less than forty-five minutes ago that we'd let them out of the building. Was that really possible? So much had happened since we'd come back upstairs to tell them all we were leaving and get the secret of how to open the door from Jason so we could make our escape. It was hard to believe that so little time had passed since then, but at least it gave us a firm timeline. We could even shave some time off of that, since Jason's body had been cold to the touch when we'd found him. I remembered my fingertips on his throat as I'd searched for a pulse, and how chilled his skin had been. Jake and I had left with the caterers at ten after seven, and we'd returned to the penthouse half an hour later. That left a tight window, but there was one huge problem with the scenario: Jake and I had both been away when the murder had occurred. That meant that we would have to rely on our witnesses for a great deal of our information, and if I'd learned anything in the past, it was that recollections could be wrong, no matter how recent. Also, the murderer would have no incentive to tell us the truth.

That left us both a great deal of detecting to do if we were going to find the killer.

"Excuse me," Candida said, bringing my attention back to our conversation. "You seemed to have lost interest in our conversation. I'm sorry. Am I boring you?" It appeared that would be a capital crime, at least in her mind.

"Sorry about that. I was just considering the possibilities," I said. "So, do you have an alibi from seven ten to seven forty?"

"I was with Bernard the entire time. He can vouch for me, and I can testify that he was with me, as well," she said.

"I'm sure that he'll alibi you, too. Did anyone else happen to see either of you the entire time?"

Candida frowned for a split second, and that's when I knew that I'd struck pay dirt. I decided to push her while her companion was still being grilled by my husband. "When did you two split up, Candida? You might as well tell me, because if you don't, I'm sure that someone else will. This place isn't big enough to do anything without someone else noticing."

Candida looked as though she was ready to take her chances that it wouldn't happen, but after a moment's hesitation, she finally admitted, "That dreadful Hazel pulled me aside to get my opinion on interior design. I tried to shake her off, but she is like some kind of tick. When I finally shed myself of her, I looked up and saw...well, never mind what I saw."

"You might as well tell me all of it." I pushed her a little harder.

"What are you talking about so earnestly, ladies?" Bernard asked as he joined us. "Candida, do you have a moment?"

She couldn't have looked any guiltier if she'd had actual blood on her hands. "Of course. We were just discussing the weather."

Candida glanced at me, begging me to back her up. I wasn't in the habit of lying to or for strangers, but then again, if I got her on my side, maybe she'd be an asset to me later. "Tell us, what do you think, Bernard? Do you believe the ice storm is going to hit us full force, or will it turn into rain pretty soon? If you ask me, I'm betting on rain," I said.

"How on earth could I possibly have an informed opinion about that? I'm not a meteorologist, and neither is my date for the weekend. Now, if you'll excuse us," he said, taking his companion's arm in his and walking her over to the windows. It was clear Candida had no choice in the matter.

"Jake doesn't want you talking," I reminded them both.

Neither one deigned to answer me, which I suppose was answer enough.

There was only one person Candida would hesitate to incriminate, and that had to be her date, Bernard Mallory. Where exactly had she seen him emerge? From Jason and Elizabeth's suite, perhaps? Was it possible that Bernard had ignored his own best interests and gotten rid of Jason in spite of the fact that it would hurt his financial situation? I wasn't sure, but I needed to speak with Jake to see what he thought about the possibility.

My husband was emerging from the suite area when I caught him before he could summon his next suspect. "I need a second."

"Okay, but that's about all I've got," Jake said as he watched everyone in the room suddenly watching us. "What's up?"

In a soft voice only loud enough for him to hear, I asked him, "Did Bernard mention that he was with Candida during the time of the murder, or did he admit that they got separated for a bit? By the way, the timeline has to be between seven ten and seven forty."

"Yes, I worked that out as well," Jake said with a slight smile. "It's true, Bernard told me that he went to their suite alone to get his medications for the night. Evidently he's on several different prescriptions for hypertension, and he said if he didn't take them at the right time, he'd feel a little off for days. He was reluctant to admit it to me at first, but I finally wore him down. Evidently no one knows he's taking meds, not even Candida."

That would certainly explain why he hadn't taken her along with him, but why keep it such a secret from her? A lot of people had high blood pressure, but they didn't find the need to hide it. Then again, I was guessing that Bernard had to present a strong front to the world, or people might think he was weak and try to take advantage of him.

It all seemed silly to me, but in his world, it might have just been true.

"Okay. She told me that he slipped away while Hazel grilled her about interior decorating, and when she looked up, he was just rejoining everyone else."

"So I don't need to speak with Candida. Thanks, that will help," Jake said with a nod. "Keep up the good work."

"Who are you going to speak with next?" I asked him.

"I haven't quite made up my mind yet, so I'm open to suggestions," he admitted.

"I'd talk to Cheyenne if I were you. Death by blunt force trauma seems right up her alley."

"Are you sure you don't want to save her for yourself?" he asked.

"No, be my guest. She's all yours."

"Okay, I'll take her. Who are you going to tackle next?"

I looked around the room and noticed that out of all of them, Joan was the only one to even pretend that she wasn't watching our every move. Her desire to be inconspicuous caught my attention immediately. "I want to speak with Joan."

"Really?" Jake asked, clearly surprised by my choice. "She seems harmless enough to me."

"I don't know why, so don't ask me to explain myself. Let's just call it a hunch."

"That's good enough for me," Jake said as he touched my cheek lightly. "You've got good instincts. Trust them."

"Yes, sir," I said with a grin.

"I'm serious, Suzanne."

"So am I. We can catch up after you finish with Cheyenne. One thing, though."

"What's that?" Jake asked, already distracted, thinking about what his line of questioning would be for Jason's suspected lover.

"Don't get caught up in her charm and let her beguile you," I said quite seriously.

Jake shook his head as he grinned. "There's only one woman in the world I want to be beguiled by, and I'm looking right at her," he said as he stared into my eyes.

"And don't you forget it," I said, and then I gave him a quick kiss just in case he needed a reminder.

He didn't, but it was fun, anyway.

"Cheyenne, do you have a minute?" he asked her.

She was clearly startled by being called next and just as obviously not happy about it. "Are you sure you want to talk to *me*? I don't know a thing," she said.

"Then it shouldn't take long," Jake said with the hint of a smile.

"Oh, fine. I'm coming," she replied as she glanced back at Joan for a second. Did she shake her head quickly, or had it been my imagination? I had to wonder if she was warning her coworker about something or if it had just been my mind playing tricks on me.

I didn't know for sure, but I was about to find out.

It was time to put a little pressure on the woman and see if I could get the truth out of her.

"Please don't," Joan said as I approached her. She looked as though she'd rather do anything but speak to me, but sadly for her, she wasn't going to get a choice.

"Don't what? I just want to ask you a few questions."

"Ms. Hart, I didn't kill Mr. Martin!" Her voice had gotten shrill and loud. Everyone was looking at us, and they weren't even trying to hide their interest in what had set her off.

"Let's start over, shall we? Take a deep breath and try to relax, Joan," I said. "And by the way, I'm Suzanne, not Ms. Hart."

"Okay," Joan said as she lowered her voice. "Suzanne it is. I meant what I said. I didn't kill him. The truth is that I didn't really even know him very well. It really surprised me when he asked me to come this weekend. Honestly, it wasn't really a request. It was more of an order."

"Do you think that he really *just* invited you along to explain his financial situation?" I asked her. It was an innocent enough question, but it certainly got a reaction from her.

"Why? What have you heard? You can't listen to office gossip. I *never* had a personal relationship with him, no matter what anybody might have said to the contrary. Well, not for a long time, anyway."

I hadn't been digging all that hard, and I'd clearly already hit a sore spot. "Joan, you need to tell me all about it. Trust me, not only will it do you good, but it's going to come out eventually anyway. After all, the man was murdered tonight."

"Don't you think I know that?" she asked in a hushed whisper. "I've been dreading the day Cheyenne found out about us. She's going to literally lose her mind when she hears," Joan whispered as she kept glancing over at Elizabeth. "Do you think she knows, too? Of course she does! How could she not have heard what happened? What am I going to do?"

"What exactly was the nature of your relationship?" I asked her, trying to be as calm as I could about it.

"It was at the office Christmas party five years ago," Joan admitted as a blush spread across her cheeks. "The alcohol was flowing pretty freely, and Mr. Martin found me at my desk working. It wasn't like I hadn't been celebrating, too, but I had a thought about how to handle a tricky amortization problem I'd been having, and I wanted to jot down a few notes so I wouldn't forget it the next day. I was leaning over my desk writing when he came up behind me and kissed me."

"And then what happened?" I asked.

"Nothing, I swear it! Okay, I might have kissed him back, but only for a few seconds. When I realized that I was kissing a married man, I pulled away and slapped his face, and I mean hard. I thought he was going to fire me on the spot, but he just laughed. We never spoke of it again, but we both knew what happened that night."

I'd been expecting much worse. While I didn't condone women going around kissing married men, it wasn't exactly a full-blown affair, either. I had a feeling that the reason Jason hadn't ever mentioned it to her was because he probably hadn't even remembered doing it in the first place. No doubt he'd been drunk, and it wouldn't have surprised me if he'd made a pass at Mrs. Claus herself that night. Was *that* why Joan had been looking so guilty? It wasn't exactly a moment of her life that she could proudly point to, but then again, was it cause for murder? I had a hard time believing it, especially since it had happened so long ago.

"You won't tell her, will you?" Joan pled with me.

"I don't see any reason to hurt Elizabeth with the information at this point," I admitted.

"I'm not talking about her. Well, her too, but I mainly meant Cheyenne. She cannot find out!"

There was a stab of fear in her voice as she said it, and it was enough to catch my attention. "Joan, are you afraid of Cheyenne?"

"You don't know what she's like! She's got a horrible temper! Did you know that she's been arrested in the past for threatening old boyfriends? I've heard stories around the office that confirm that she doesn't take being scorned lightly."

"Do you think she might have actually killed Jason?" I asked her softly.

"I don't know," she said, her voice clearly on the edge of hysteria. "We were hanging out together while you and your husband were gone, but I lost track of her for a few minutes at some point. How long does it take to kill someone? I heard someone talking earlier. The killer hit him in the head, isn't that right?"

"Yes," I admitted.

"How awful. He wasn't exactly the best person in the world to work for, but he didn't deserve that. You and your husband need to figure out who did it."

"We're doing our best," I said. "Did you happen to speak with anyone while Cheyenne was off somewhere else by herself?"

"I was talking to Mrs. Jackson at one point," she admitted. "I spotted her coming out of the suite area, and we made eye contact for just an instant. She seemed flushed, and her voice was kind of all in a twitter when she spoke."

"What did you two happen to talk about?" I asked her.

"Her hand," Joan said.

"Her hand? What about it?"

"It looked to me as though she had cut her palm on something," Joan said. "She had a guest washcloth wrapped around it, and there was some blood on it. I hate blood."

That was interesting. "Did she happen to say how she injured herself?"

"She tried to make light of it, like she was so clumsy that she was constantly hurting herself, but I'm not sure that I believed her."

I looked over at Lara and saw that she'd been watching us intently. The moment we made eye contact, she looked away, but it was too late.

I'd seen the fear in her expression about what Joan might be divulging to me.

"Thank you so much. You've been a big help," I said as I started to walk toward Lara Jackson.

I didn't make it, though. Joan put a hand on my shoulder, and I was surprised by how strong she was. I'd been about to discount her involvement, but she was pretty intense as she spoke. "Don't tell anyone what I told you!"

"I *have* to share it with my husband," I told her, trying to pry off her hand. "He's conducting the investigation, and it's valuable information."

"How is what I did so long ago important now?" Joan asked me.

"Whether we like it or not, we have to consider everyone here a suspect," I explained to her.

"Me? You think I could have done it?" she asked, her voice suddenly getting loud again.

Anyone who hadn't been watching us before was certainly paying attention to us now.

"I'm not saying that at all," I said loudly so everyone there could hear me, too.

That seemed to mollify her a little, even though I hadn't told her what she'd clearly thought I had. I wasn't discounting her from consideration, but I had a hunch that's the way she'd taken it. "Okay, but I can't risk Cheyenne finding out about what happened," Joan said, her voice starting to tremble a little again.

I finally got myself free of her grasp. "I'll do what I can to protect your secret from everyone else, but I can't make any promises."

"I'm not sure that's good enough," she said, narrowing her gaze at me.

There was nothing else I could say to ease her concerns, and I wasn't sure that I wanted to, anyway. She was a suspect just as much as everyone else there was. "I really do need to go," I told her as I glanced back in Lara's direction.

The only problem was that she was gone.

Why had she left in such a hurry, and really, where was there to go?

CHAPTER 14

"WHERE DO YOU THINK YOU'RE going?" I asked Lara Jackson as I spotted her heading for the penthouse exit door.

"Things are getting a little close in here," she said as she took her hand from the doorknob as though it were on fire. "I thought I'd step out and get a breath of fresh air."

"I'm sorry, but you need to stay here with everyone else," I reminded her. I looked down at her hand. It was no longer wrapped in the washcloth Joan had seen. Now she had a silk scarf tied around it, as though she were trying to make some kind of fashion statement instead of hiding her wounds. I pretended to notice it accidentally. "What happened to your hand?"

"I scraped it leaning against the fireplace, okay?" she asked with a hiss. "Have you seen the sharp corners on those stones? I knew that blabbermouth would say something to you. What did she tell you?"

"Nothing that might necessarily concern you," I lied, "but it seems curious that you're reacting so aggressively at the moment. I just asked you a simple question."

"I'm on edge, okay?" she asked after she took a few measured breaths. The woman was good at gathering her composure quickly. "Everyone here knows that I didn't exactly worship the ground that Jason walked on. You all heard me berate him earlier, and now he's dead. I'm not stupid, Suzanne. I know how it looks."

She referred to his demise almost as though it had been the victim's fault that he'd been murdered, as though it was an inconvenience for her, instead of a tragic end for him. "When was the last time you saw him alive?" I asked her.

"Why do you want to know that?" Lara asked me.

"Well, besides the fact that we're asking everyone that question, it's a legitimate request. As you just said, you two were arguing in front of all of us, and now he's dead. Why *wouldn't* we want to talk to you about what happened to him?"

"I didn't kill him!" she said, her face flushing for just a moment. I didn't know about Jake, but I was getting a great many reactions to what seemed on the surface like simple questions that I was posing. It was almost as though the people gathered together couldn't wait to deny the fact that they'd killed one of our hosts.

"I never said that you did. However, you never answered my question. When was the last time you saw Jason Martin alive?" I asked, reminding her that she wasn't going to get the chance to duck my question with histrionics.

"I saw him just after you and your husband left," she finally admitted. "We had words, as I'm sure Joan told you earlier, so don't act so surprised."

It was my turn to be legitimately startled by her statement. "She told me that she saw you coming out of the suite area, but she never said anything about you being with Jason just before he died, let alone that you two were arguing about something."

"Because it didn't mean anything!" Lara snapped.

Everyone else there was watching us with great interest again. I hadn't had so much attention paid to me since I'd played a daisy in the grade school spring play. "Why should I believe you?"

"Because it's the truth," she said. "I saw Jason in the hallway, and it's true that we had a few words, but that was it. If you don't believe me, you can ask Hazel. She came looking for Jason as I was storming off, and she looked thoroughly upset about something. If you ask me, *she* should be at the top of your list!"

"What really happened to your hand, Lara?" I asked, pushing her even harder. I didn't believe her story about the fireplace stones. She had tried too hard to act nonchalant as she'd told me the story. Clearly something else had happened, and I meant to find out the truth.

"I told you earlier, I scraped it on the fireplace stones," she repeated, her gaze darting downward and avoiding mine for a split second.

"Are you sure it didn't happen when you grabbed the murder weapon and killed Jason? I need to know exactly what happened," I said calmly. I wasn't about to back down. One way or the other, I was going to get the truth out of her.

After a full twenty seconds of awkward silence, she finally spoke. "Okay, I was lying about the fireplace before," she said, looking incredibly guilty. "I just didn't want anyone to know what really happened."

"Go on. You can tell me," I said in my most sympathetic voice. Was I about to get an impromptu murder confession?

"I broke a glass, okay? I was so mad about Jason blowing me off that I had to go into the bathroom to collect myself. They have crystal in there! Can you believe it? My husband and I had to take a second mortgage out on our house just to pay our bills, and they are throwing a party with crystal in the bathroom!"

Henry came over at last to see why his wife was so agitated. "Is everything okay here?"

"It's fine," Lara said, doing her best to keep her voice calm.

"What did you do to your hand?" her husband asked her.

"I cut it on some broken glass," she admitted. "It's nothing, really."

"Let's go to the bathroom so I can look at it," he insisted.

Before they could take a step though, I said, "Sorry, but I need to go first." I jumped ahead of them and went in, locking the door behind me. I wasn't about to let her break a glass after her confession just to "prove" that she'd really cut her hand in there and not in the master suite committing murder.

When I searched the place though, I didn't see any evidence of a broken crystal tumbler.

The trash can was empty, and there wasn't much space to hide something in the powder room. To be thorough though, I opened the vanity door and saw something pushed all the way toward the back.

It was a washcloth with a bit of blood on it.

Grabbing a hand towel, I reached in and pulled it out.

Sure enough, a shattered crystal tumbler was inside the loose folds, and there were a few drops of blood on some of the pieces.

It appeared that Lara had been telling the truth, about that, at any rate.

But that didn't make her innocent of murder. She could have cut her hand on the geode bookend and then staged the glass breakage to cover her tracks. It would have been a clever move, but I was on to her.

As things stood, it was just another piece of information to file away. I decided not to return the broken glass to its hiding spot, and as I opened the door, I had the washcloth secured in the crook of my arm.

"I don't think you're supposed to take those out of the restroom," Hazel said as she met me.

"I need it for something," I told her.

She didn't even push me on it. "Suzanne, we need to talk."

"That was my sentiment exactly," I said. "I was just about to come looking for you."

"Why do you need to speak with me?" she asked me quizzically.

"I understand that you had hard words with Jason just before he died," I said, doing my best to watch her expression as I said it. She was a good friend of mine, someone I liked and admired, but that didn't exempt her from our investigation. I knew firsthand that sometimes killers could be nice people pushed into extraordinary situations. Just because Hazel was a friend didn't give her a free pass. I needed to push her just as hard as I did our other suspects, no matter what it might do to our friendship later if she turned out to be innocent. I'd lost friends before in the course of my investigations, but no matter how much it pained me, I couldn't let that stop me from pursuing the truth.

Hazel was taken aback by my statement. She wanted to be angry, I could see it in her eyes, but after a moment, the irritation segued into resignation.

"You're right. We might as well get this over with. I need to tell you the truth."

Was my friend about to confess to murder right then and there? "Did you do it, Hazel?" I asked her softly, hoping against hope that it wasn't true.

"Did I what? Kill him? Don't be ridiculous," she replied. After a moment's thought, she added, "Given the circumstances, I don't suppose it's that ridiculous a question after all. No, I was angry enough to slap him hard in the face, but I never would have killed the man. It was awful finding him like that, wasn't it?"

It had been quite a bit worse for Jason, but I knew what she meant. "If you didn't kill him, then what exactly did you want to tell me?"

"Just that I slapped his face and told him that he didn't deserve Elizabeth," Hazel said. "It wasn't a love tap, either. I hit him hard enough to get his attention, and it left an angry red mark on his cheek! I couldn't believe he had the gall to bring his mistress to the party!"

Was that his greatest sin in her eyes, when he'd seemed to

commit so many others? "How did he react to your slap?" I asked her.

"He laughed at me! The truth is that it made me even more furious with him," Hazel admitted, her eyes blazing for a moment.

"What did you do then?"

"Given the circumstances, I'm not sure what I *would* have done, but Jennifer came in at the very end and witnessed the last bit. She grabbed me and pulled me out of that bedroom suite before I could do anything else. I was angry with her at the time for butting in, but now I'm glad that she cared enough to do it."

I supposed that it was an alibi of sorts, but I needed confirmation. I looked around for Jennifer to see if I could ask her, but she was nowhere in sight. Why did people keep disappearing when Jake and I had asked them to stay in one place?

Hazel must have read my mind. "If you're looking for Jennifer, she's back talking to Jake."

"I didn't even see him come out after he spoke with Cheyenne," I admitted.

"He was just here for a second," Hazel admitted. "We need to figure out how to get out of here, Suzanne. Elizabeth is close to breaking down."

"Shouldn't you be with her, then?" I asked her. It was spoken more out of compassion for our mutual friend than my role as an assistant in the investigation, but sometimes I needed to be a friend, too.

"You're right. I'm going to go to her now," Hazel said, and then she was gone, not even looking back in my direction.

I'd learned more than I'd expected, but my thoughts were just as confused as ever. I hoped Jake was getting a little clarity from his part of our investigation, and I couldn't wait to compare notes with him. So far, it seemed that no one was exempted from our suspicion.

I was about to go looking for Jake when we lost our backup power, too.

Instantly, the entire room was plunged in darkness.

I'd only thought that everything had been bathed in shadows before.

But I'd been wrong.

Now the entire room was pitch black.

At least the total darkness was brief.

After a few moments, the lights came back on in all of their glory.

The brightness stung my eyes, and as I recovered my vision, I looked around to see how everyone else was reacting to the sudden influx of light.

The scene was rather illuminating.

Bernard had Candida by the arm, and she was wincing from the tightness of his grip. She looked terrified by her companion, and I wondered what had just transpired between them. Lara was inching her way toward the door to the vestibule, while her husband was clearly looking for her over by the bar. She looked guilty when we made eye contact, and I had to wonder if she'd been trying to slip away yet again. The three women in my book club had been gathered together on one of the sofas, and they were looking at each other as though one of them had just said something shocking, while Cheyenne and Joan were missing entirely. Were they in their suite, or had they already made their escape in the darkness? I realized they were still in their room when Cheyenne came barreling out of the suite area with Joan fast on her heels just as the main lights died again and we were forced to get by with backup lighting only.

"What was that all about?" Cheyenne asked. "Is it gone again already? I thought we were going to have power again."

"It was just a surge," Jake said.

"I thought you were a cop, not an electrician," Lara said, her face a little flushed.

"Hey, I know things," Jake answered with a shrug.

"So do I," Cheyenne said.

"About electricity?" Henry asked.

"No, about our hostess," she said.

"You need to be very careful about what you say next," Elizabeth said as she started to stand. Hazel and Jennifer immediately stood to stop her, but I wasn't sure that even the two of them could manage it given Elizabeth's expression.

"Why, are you going to sic your goons on me?" Cheyenne asked. "You are weak and pathetic, and what's worse, you don't even know it! You don't even realize that I've got a part of Jason that you can never take away from me, and I'm certainly not afraid of your entourage of middle-aged hags."

"Who are you calling middle aged?" Hazel asked, displaying a flare of temper I hadn't known she'd possessed. It was interesting to me that she hadn't objected to being called a hag but to being categorized as middle aged.

Now it was Elizabeth's turn to restrain her friend. After Hazel was calmer, Elizabeth said icily, "You know nothing about me."

"That's what you think."

"I'm curious. What do you think you know?"

"Plenty. For instance, I know that Jason told me that he was afraid you were going to try to kill him," Cheyenne said.

"Take that back! That's a lie," Elizabeth snarled. She was still grieving the loss of her husband, and her emotions were all on the surface.

"We both know that it's true, and I won't be bullied by the likes of you," Cheyenne said as she turned to Jake. "Ask her about the insurance policy she made Jason take out on his life a few weeks ago."

"You don't know what you're talking about," Elizabeth said. "It was his idea, not mine."

"That's not what he told us," Cheyenne said.

"Us?" Jennifer asked her.

"Joan knew about it, too," Cheyenne said. "Go on, ask her. Joan, tell them," she urged as she turned to her coworker.

"I had to process the check," Joan explained almost apologetically.

"That covers the fact that there was a new insurance policy taken out but not whose idea it was originally," Hazel said.

"Mr. Martin told me jokingly that he was worried about why his wife suddenly wanted to insure him," Joan admitted. "I'm so sorry," she said as she apologized to the recent widow.

"I never said or did any such thing!" Elizabeth said loudly.

"You can deny it all you want, but that doesn't make it so," Cheyenne said tauntingly.

"That's enough, ladies," Bernard said. "Things are bad enough without the two of you squabbling."

"Don't pretend you didn't want him dead, too," Henry Jackson said. His outburst surprised me. So far I'd thought him to be a rather meek member of the party, but he was obviously furious now.

"That's ludicrous," Bernard said.

"There's no use denying it. I heard you two arguing earlier," Henry explained, not backing down under the man's glare.

"I don't know what you're talking about," Bernard answered, trying to blow the claim off.

"Maybe I should refresh your memory then. You told him that if he didn't have the interest payment he owed you by Monday morning, you'd break him down to nothing and make him wish he were never born."

Bernard looked at Henry as though he was a mosquito buzzing around his head. "I admit that we had words, and it is true that Jason was late with his payments, but as I told the inspector earlier, I needed the man alive if I were ever going to recoup my initial investment."

"Is that what they're calling loansharking these days?" Henry asked defiantly.

"You, sir, need to watch your tongue," Bernard said as he took a step toward Henry. "You had more reason to kill our host than I did. He lost your life savings, didn't he?"

"It was a deal that went bad. I keep telling everyone that it wasn't Jason's fault."

Bernard shrugged off his response and turned to Lara instead. "Is that how you feel about it, Mrs. Jackson?"

"No, of course not, but it was only money. I wouldn't kill anyone because of it, even him."

"So you say," Candida replied, trying to back up Bernard's attack.

From where I was standing, I couldn't tell who was more annoyed by her interjection, the Jacksons or Bernard Mallory.

"Stay out of this, Candida," Bernard told her.

"You know that you don't have to let him talk to you that way, don't you?" Joan asked, surprising everyone by coming to Candida's defense. First she'd tried to help Cheyenne, and now she was doing her best to support Candida.

"Do you *truly* want to involve yourself in this?" Bernard asked her with a wicked smile. "What happened, did Jason rebuff your advances and you punished him for it?"

Joan's face reddened, and two women in particular looked at her harshly at the same time. I was certain that Cheyenne and Elizabeth had both been surprised by the accusation, based on their mirror expressions. "It never happened."

"So you say," Bernard answered.

"What about that group over there?" Lara asked as she

pointed to the three members of the book club. "Maybe they all did it together."

"That's ridiculous," Elizabeth said. "My friends are here to support me."

"Fine. If you didn't *all* do it, maybe *one* of you did it to protect your friend," Lara replied.

I wasn't about to admit it, but that possibility had certainly crossed my mind as well. Was it *really* possible, though? I'd spent quality time with those ladies, and the idea that one of them might be a murderer turned my stomach. Still, Jake and I couldn't just dismiss the possibility because of our friendships.

Speaking of Jake, he chose that moment to walk over to me and ask softly, "Suzanne, are you okay?"

"I'm a little shaky, to be honest with you. They're turning on each other like rats on a sinking ship, aren't they? How did the rest of your interviews go?"

"Cheyenne has a wicked temper, Henry certainly has his own reason, no matter how much he might deny it, and Jennifer seems like the type of woman who would have no trouble killing someone threatening her friend. The fact of the matter is that everyone here had a reason to hate Jason. I'm frankly amazed that he lived as long as he did with so many enemies."

"Poor Elizabeth. Look at her over there. I'm so worried about her." My friend was staring off into space at the moment, completely lost in her own thoughts and oblivious to the current arguments.

"You realize that you can't let your emotions rule you right now," Jake reminded me.

"I know. It's hard, though. Those women are my friends."

"I understand completely. Suzanne, I need you to do something for me while they are engaging in tearing each other down."

"Anything. All you have to do is ask. You know that."

He patted my shoulder gently. "I knew I could count on you.

While they are all distracted, why don't you slip away and do a quick search of the suites? I'd love to go with you, but things might turn ugly here, and I have to be able to step in if that happens. Are you okay doing it alone?"

"Are you telling me that I need to search Elizabeth and Jason's suite too?" I asked, remembering what the dead man had looked like when we'd first found him.

"If you don't want to do it, I understand," Jake said.

"No, I agree. It needs to be done. Are you sure you trust *me* to do it? You're trained for this sort of thing, not me."

"Don't sell yourself short," he said with a brief grin. "Now go on before they notice that you're gone. Good luck."

"You, too," I said as I moved back into the shadows and made my way to the suites we were all occupying.

It was time to do a quick recon and see if I could find any evidence that might help us figure out who had killed our host while Jake monitored the flaring tempers in the main area. His job was undoubtedly the more dangerous of the two, but if I got caught riffling through other people's things, I might be the one in jeopardy.

The answer was simple, even if it was going to be hard to pull off.

I needed to be quick, thorough, and stealthy, all at the same time.

It was going to be harder than it sounded, and it sounded nearly impossible, but I was going to do my best not to let my husband down.

Unfortunately, I didn't get a chance to do anything just yet, though.

I was about to slip away when I heard someone suddenly start sobbing and screaming at the same time.

I'd been wondering when the enormity of our situation was going to make someone crack.

I just hadn't expected it to be Candida.

CHAPTER 15

"**W**HY ARE WE ALL JUST standing around calmly as though nothing happened tonight?" she started yelling. "A man is dead, and whether we liked him or not, we can't just do *nothing*! Why isn't someone going for help?"

"Get a grip on yourself," Bernard said sternly as he stared at his companion. "The inspector is doing all that he can, given the circumstances." It was unusual to say the least to have the criminal come to the defense of the cop.

"I won't! If you won't do something, then I will!" She started toward the penthouse door when Bernard's hand lashed out with a quickness I never would have expected from him. She recoiled as though his grip had been on fire. "Get your hands off me! You've touched me for the last time!"

"I know you're upset, but you need to watch yourself very carefully right now," Bernard said with a coldness in his voice that chilled me to my core.

"I won't!" She raced for the exit, but Jake was there one step ahead of her. He quickly moved in front of her to block her escape.

In calm tones, he said, "Candida, we're all upset by what happened, but there's nothing we can do but wait. The guard will be back tomorrow morning, and all we can do is keep our heads until he returns. The truth of the matter is that unless the power comes back on, nobody's going anywhere."

"Why aren't you doing something about that, then? You claim to have been a cop. Do something!" she shouted.

"I'm doing everything in my power," Jake said. He looked around for someone to step in and comfort her, and I started toward her before Jake glanced in my direction and shook his head quickly. He then made a darting motion with his eyes that told me I should go now, while everyone else was distracted by Candida's outburst. I knew in my heart that he was right, but it was difficult not going to someone's aid when they were clearly in need of comforting.

"Joan, could you give me a hand here?" Jake asked.

The accountant looked startled, and more than a little bit pleased, to be called on for help. "Of course," she said. As she approached Candida, she paused long enough to give Bernard one quick and withering look. Wrapping her arm around Candida's shoulder, Joan said, "Come on. Let's get you something to drink. Would you like some coffee, or maybe something stronger?"

"I *hate* coffee," she said, which was odd coming from a former barista. Then again, maybe that was *why* she didn't like the drink anymore. I'd had a friend in high school who had worked one summer at an old-fashioned ice cream parlor, and by the time September rolled around, she couldn't even look a scoop of vanilla in the eye.

"Then something stronger it is," Joan said.

That was the last bit of their conversation I heard. While just about everyone else was occupied with comforting Candida, I crept off to the bedroom suites to see if I could find any evidence that might be able to help uncover who had killed Jason Martin right under our very noses.

My cell phone battery was getting low from using it so much as a flashlight, so I was going to have to use it sparingly from now on, though it was going to inhibit my search. I decided that Jake and I had already searched Elizabeth and Jason's suite, which suited me just fine. If I had to, I'd go back there at the end, but at the moment, I had no desire to go back into the room where the body was lying. I decided to take Bernard and Candida's room first, since there was no telling when they might come back, given the woman's earlier outburst. Not that I could blame her. I felt exactly the same way inside, and this was by no means my first body.

The suite was immaculate, which didn't surprise me, given Bernard's neat attire. I suspected he would settle for nothing else. At least it made it easy to search their room. I didn't see anything out of the ordinary on first glance, with the exception of a locked briefcase someone had slid under the bed. I pulled it out to see if I could open it, but it was a mini fortress, made from steel instead of leather, with a combination lock that was well beyond my ability to open. What was so valuable that he had to treat it like gold? For all I knew it could have *been* gold, but not much of it, given the case's weight. The briefcase itself was heavy, and I couldn't detect a great deal of weight beyond that, so I figured it must be filled with paperwork, which could be valuable in and of itself. Not that it would do me any good. I put the case back where I'd found it, and then I went off to search Lara and Henry's room. I just hoped I had better luck there.

The suite the Jacksons had taken over was a mess, the polar opposite of what I'd found in Bernard's bedroom. I started looking through their open suitcases, and I was about to give up when I found a large white envelope tucked away in the bottom of Lara's bag. Pulling the documentation out, I read a bit of it when I realized that it was a notice of eviction from their home. They were being foreclosed on! Was Henry even aware of it, or had she hidden it from him? It certainly confirmed that they were in financial straits, but why bring it with them for the weekend? Was she honestly going to try to shame Jason into bailing them out? If that had been her intention, I couldn't imagine the tactic working. Jason had seemed to me like a man mostly uninfluenced by pleas of the heart.

The next suite I searched was the last one, Joan and Cheyenne's area. One side of the room was neat as a pin, while the other had clothes strewn all about it. It didn't take long for me to figure out that Joan was the slob, not Cheyenne, something that surprised me, based on what I knew of their personalities. I did a quick look around Joan's space without finding anything significant, and then I studied Cheyenne's area.

There was nothing of significance that I could find there either, and I was about to give up when I walked into the bathroom to look around, just as I had the other suites.

I was about to write that off as well when I realized that something was buried in the bottom of the trashcan, wrapped up in way too many tissues.

It was a pregnancy test, and what was more, the plus sign indicating a positive result was quite apparent.

Evidently one of the two women was pregnant, and given what I knew of their behavior, I had a suspicion that it was Cheyenne who had tested positive. Had she confronted Jason with the results, expecting him to leave Elizabeth? I could see her doing it, just as easily as I could imagine Jason laughing at her in response.

A rebuff at a time like that would certainly give her a reason to kill him in a fit of rage.

Now all I had to do was figure out how to show Jake without tipping my hand to the others.

When I got back out into the main living space of the penthouse, I heard people yelling. It appeared that everyone was arguing with everyone else, and accusations were flying around like bats in a cave at dusk. Why was Jake letting them carry on like that? And then I realized that there was method to his madness. If he let them fight among themselves, there would be less chance that someone would notice my absence in the ruckus.

My husband made his way over to me quickly, and as he did, he whispered, "Did you find anything we can use?"

"Lara had a notice of foreclosure on their home, but that's not the real bombshell. I found a positive pregnancy test in Joan and Cheyenne's bathroom."

"Good work. Did you happen to keep it?" he asked.

"It's in my pocket. Why, do you want to see it?"

"No, I just want to make sure we've got it," he replied. "Let's go ask Joan and Cheyenne about it. One of them might have a stronger motive than the others to have killed Jason."

"I'm not pregnant," Joan said loudly just after Jake asked her in a gentle voice. "Frankly, I resent you accusing me of being in that state. Regardless of what you might think of me, my mother didn't raise a tramp."

I wasn't about to stand there debating moral codes with her. "That's all we wanted to know," I said soothingly. I looked at Jake, who wasn't watching me at all. He was looking quickly around the dark room, and it only took me a second to realize what he was doing. "Where's Cheyenne?" I asked aloud, wondering where she'd gotten herself off to.

"That's what I want to know," Jake said softly to me. In a louder voice, he said, "Can I have your attention, please? Quiet!" The last bit had been shouted, and everyone suddenly did as my husband ordered. There was something in his tone that had a note of authority in it, and he'd once told me that it was his "cop's voice," something that had come with being on the force for so long. Once he had everyone's attention, he asked, "Has anyone seen Cheyenne?"

They all looked surprised by the question as they started looking all around the room.

"She's not here," Bernard said, stating the obvious.

"Where could she go, though?" Joan asked. "We're all trapped here."

"Just because she's not in this room doesn't mean that she got away," Jennifer said. "Don't forget, there are twelve empty floors below us, and a lobby, too."

"Jennifer!" Elizabeth snapped at her best friend.

"Relax, Elizabeth. If they don't know it yet, they will shortly enough. It's not important right now."

"Don't forget the roof," Henry said. "She could be up there, too. We need to go find her."

"We will, but we're going to do this in an organized manner," Jake said. "I'm assigning teams of two to branch out and see if we can locate her."

"Is *she* the killer?" Elizabeth asked softly. "I knew it in my heart the moment we found my husband's body."

"We don't know *anything* yet," I said, though that clearly wasn't quite the entire truth. "We just need to stick together."

"How can we stick together if we're going to form search parties?" Lara asked. "Surely you're not suggesting we go as a group from floor to floor."

"What's wrong with that idea?" Jennifer asked. "When you think about it, it's the only way we can keep tabs on each other." She looked around the dim room as though she didn't trust any of us, including me. I'd clearly fallen out of favor with my club, but I'd have to worry about that later. At the moment, we had a member of our party to locate. "What do you think, Jake?"

"There are certainly merits to what you're suggesting, but I'd feel better if we found her sooner rather than later," he admitted.

"Why is that?" Hazel asked.

It was clear that Jake didn't want to answer, and I couldn't blame him. We didn't want to give away what might be a piece of crucial information to the others if we didn't have to. I had to wonder if Jake was thinking the same thing that I was. If Cheyenne had confronted Jason about her pregnancy, been rebuffed, and killed him in a fit of rage, she might do something to herself now. If she couldn't break out of the building, she might do something a little more drastic to make sure that she never had to face the music for her actions.

"It just makes sense," I said without providing any real reasons to my friend. It was important that I backed up Jake's call, and it helped that I actually agreed with him. I had a hunch that Cheyenne hadn't trusted us when we'd said that we'd been locked in. "Jake and I will take the lobby," I said to the group.

"Lara and I will search the roof," Henry volunteered.

Jake nodded in agreement. "Okay. How do the rest of you want to team up?"

"We're not going anywhere," Elizabeth said firmly. "That tramp's whereabouts don't matter one bit to me. Jennifer, Hazel, will you stay here with me?"

It was clear that the women had been ready to join the search party, but Elizabeth's pleas were hard to ignore. Again, I was a little hurt that she hadn't asked me to stay as well, but I couldn't let that bother me at the moment. "We aren't going anywhere without you," Jennifer assured her, shooting an apologetic look in my direction as she said it. At least they *all* weren't against me.

"Candida and I will start on the floor just below ours," Bernard said matter-of-factly.

"I'd rather go with someone else," the former barista said.

"Nonsense. Don't be foolish. You are coming with me," Bernard insisted.

"*I'll* go with you," Joan said, stepping between Bernard and Candida.

Candida nodded, and Bernard looked flummoxed by the rebellion. "Fine. Do whatever you please. I'll go alone."

"I'm afraid I can't allow that," Jake said. "This *has* to be done on the buddy system." He turned to Jennifer, Hazel, and Elizabeth. "Would one of you like to volunteer?"

Jennifer glanced at Elizabeth for approval, who nodded once. "I'll go with you, Bernard," she said. I was glad that she'd been the one to agree. I doubted that Bernard would stand a chance if he tried to bully *her* around. Jennifer simply wouldn't stand for it.

"It's all settled, then. Whoever finds Cheyenne needs to be gentle with her. We're not trying to do anything but bring her back up here."

"Even if she's the killer?" Bernard asked, his voice snapping out the question.

"Why would you say something like that?" Lara asked him.

"It's obvious, isn't it? She's the *only* one of us who chose to run," Bernard said. "Doesn't that scream her guilt?"

"I tried to leave earlier myself," Candida said softly. "Just because she panicked doesn't mean that she killed our host."

Bernard looked at her bitingly before he replied. "Why don't you butt out and let the professionals analyze the situation?"

Joan clearly didn't like that. She'd taken Candida under her protection since Jake had asked her to comfort the woman, and she was taking the role seriously. Bernard had better watch himself. Joan was showing a maternal side to her personality that I hadn't seen before. She was so protective of the woman she'd just met that I had to wonder how she would react if a real friend of hers was threatened. Could she have been the one to kill Jason when he'd rejected her friend? The more I thought I knew, the more confused I got.

There was only one thing to do about that.

It was time to start searching for the missing party guest and ask her directly.

CHAPTER 16

THOSE OF US WHO WERE going to be actively searching for Cheyenne were all out in the hallway when Henry and Lara headed up the stairs. After a moment, the rest of us started working our way down.

"Jake, I'm not sure about our plan after all," I said quietly as we all reached the twelfth floor.

"I know it's not ideal, but what choice do we have?" he asked me as he held back a step.

"The floors are all empty between here and the ground level, right?" I asked.

"That's what we've been told, but I haven't seen that for myself," he answered.

"Then they'll be easy enough to search, won't they? I'm starting to think we should all stick together." I lowered my voice as I added, "One of us is the killer, but what if it wasn't Cheyenne? If it was someone else, we're putting someone at risk pairing them up with a murderer."

"That's a good point," Jake said. "Excuse me, everyone," he said louder. "We've had a change in plans."

"We're not going to search at all now?" Joan asked. "We need to find Cheyenne."

"And we are, but I'm beginning to think we should all stick together after all," Jake answered. "Actually, it was Jennifer's idea, and I think it's a good one. Let's all go in and check out the twelfth floor together. If it's empty, it shouldn't take us long to work our way down through the building." As Jake opened the door to the twelfth floor, I could see that it was indeed devoid of all furniture. Shoot, there weren't even any walls. The floor was almost entirely empty except for a few boxes that would hardly be big enough to hide a soul.

"I'm curious about something. Who told you that all of the floors were empty?" Candida asked Jake.

"Lara Jackson," I answered for him.

"How did she know? Did she search them all herself? That's odd, isn't it? Did Henry go with her?"

"Speaking of Henry and Lara, should someone go upstairs and get them, too?" Jennifer asked. "They're the only ones searching not with us right now."

I just shrugged in response. They were a married couple, so I wasn't too worried about them being together. Then again, if something happened to either one of them, I'd feel awful about it.

Jake nodded. "You're right. In for a penny and all that. I'll go up and get them," he said. "While I'm gone, the rest of you spread out and see if you can find any sign of Cheyenne on the eleventh floor."

I followed him into the hallway as everyone else started down the stairs. "I don't like you being by yourself," I said.

"*One* of us needs to stay here with the group," he replied. "You can go if you'd rather, but I'm armed, so if I run into trouble, I'll be better suited to handle it. You don't disagree with that, do you?"

"Of course not," I said. "I'm just not happy being away from you."

"I won't be long. I promise," he said as he smiled at me softly. "Just try to keep your eyes on everyone at once and leave the hunting to them."

"That sounds hard enough," I admitted.

"You can do it. I have faith in you."

It turned out that I didn't have to do it after all, though.

Lara Jackson came ripping down the stairs screaming for help before we could make it to the next floor!

Evidently Cheyenne had gone up instead of down after all.

CHAPTER 17

I WAS GLAD WE WERE ALL out in the stairwell. If we'd been searching another floor, I doubted that we would have heard Lara screaming. We rushed up to join her as a group while she came down the steps much too fast, tripping at the end. Thankfully Jake was there to catch her.

Once he had her steadied on her feet again, Lara explained breathlessly, "Henry is up there with her! He poked his head out the door to make sure it was safe, and he spotted her standing on the edge of the building! He said that she was threatening to jump, so he told me to get you all as quickly as I could! He's doing the best he can to stop her, but if she's determined to jump, there's nothing he's going to be able to do about it."

I was in the lead, so I tore up the steps with Jake and the rest of the group close on my heels. When we got to the door, something was partially blocking it, and we had trouble moving it at first. Jake put his shoulder into it though, and it finally opened.

I'd been hoping to see two people on the roof as we spilled out.

But unfortunately, I just saw one.

Henry was standing near the edge looking down, and I felt a kick in my gut as I joined him there. It was colder than it had been before, and the icy rain made everything slick. It was still coming down, and I felt the sting of it on my face.

As I looked down onto the ground below, I saw a body sprawled out on the sidewalk, and I knew that a fall from that high up was surely fatal. Even if we could get to Cheyenne's body, there was nothing anybody would be able to do for her.

"What happened?" Jake asked as he moved up as well, being very careful with every step.

Henry was crying as he turned to us, and he stumbled a little when he realized that we were all there. Jake reached out a hand to steady him just in time, or we might have had three fatalities that day instead of two, which was still two more than I'd wanted to see. "She said she couldn't live with the guilt," he said through his sobs. "She told me that she killed Jason when he wouldn't leave Elizabeth, and she was afraid we'd find out, so she ran up here to end it all. When Lara and I got here, Cheyenne was already standing on the edge in the rain trying to work up the nerve to jump. I told Lara to go get you while I tried to talk her into moving away from the edge. I knew that somebody needed to stay up here with her! I've never faced anything like that before. You're the professional. I couldn't stop her!" His sobs were wracking his entire body, and I worried that he might fall accidentally.

"Why don't we all go back to the penthouse where it's safe and dry?" I suggested. It was bitterly cold, and the freezing rain just made it worse. I was chilled to the bone, and I couldn't imagine how cold Henry must be.

"I tried to stop her," Henry kept repeating as we all walked him down. He had to be in shock, and I worried about his state of mind. I'd seen death close up before myself, and it was never easy, or pretty. The man would bear watching for a while to make sure that he didn't lose it completely. As his wife moved closer and hugged him, he seemed to melt against her. "I did everything I could, Lara," he said through his sobs.

"It wasn't your fault," Lara repeated as she stroked his hair. "You can't blame yourself for what happened. Come on. Let's get you inside before you catch your death."

It was the wrong word to use from an old-fashioned phrase, and the man seemed to collapse a little more in on himself when he heard it.

We were all back in the penthouse soon enough, and I was happy that there was a small natural-gas fireplace there to warm the space up. At least it hadn't been electric, which would have done us no good at all during the power outage. Henry instantly collapsed onto one of the couches, and as Lara covered him with a blanket, Candida offered to get him something to drink.

Jake said softly, "Don't give him a choice. Make it whisky," he said. "He's going to need it."

She nodded, and as she served him, Elizabeth asked, "What happened? Why is everyone so upset?"

"Cheyenne confessed to killing Jason before she jumped off the roof. She's dead," Bernard reported matter-of-factly.

"What? No. That can't be," Elizabeth said, sounding as though she were in shock herself now.

"It's all true," Henry said, and then he collapsed again into his wife's arms. I felt like some kind of voyeur watching them, but we were all trapped in a confining space. Besides, I knew that we should all be together at a time like this. The mystery of who had murdered Jason Martin might have been solved, but until we got out of our modern-day electronic prison, we needed to be there for each other.

Elizabeth looked off into the distance for a few moments, so I walked up to where she was sitting. "Are you okay? I'm sorry this nightmare just won't end for you."

It took a moment for her to register that I was even talking, and I was about to give up when she looked up, her gaze meeting mine. "Suzanne. I'm sorry."

"You have nothing to apologize to me for," I said. "You've had a great shock tonight. Two of them, actually."

"I know, but that doesn't mean that I still can't be sorry. You deserve better treatment than that. I suppose I wanted to blame you for questioning my innocence, but I didn't have any right to. You were just trying to find Jason's killer."

"It's all water under the bridge," I said. "Do you know what I think? I believe it might do us all good to get some food in us. I know the rest of you didn't eat much dinner, and I didn't finish my meal, either. Is there any chance there's anything in the kitchen that the caterers left behind? We can't cook anything elaborate, but maybe there are snacks or something we can put together."

Elizabeth nodded as she stood. Hazel got up as well, and Jennifer joined us as Elizabeth said, "The range is natural gas, just like the fireplace. There are eggs and bacon in the fridge, and if we don't cook them, they'll just end up going bad anyway."

"If you don't mind, I'd love to cook," I volunteered.

"We'll help you," Hazel said.

I called out to Jake, "We're going to make bacon and eggs. Interested?"

"It's a good idea. Is there any chance we can get some coffee, too?" he asked. It was clear that though my husband was a seasoned pro, he was still upset about the young woman's death as well. It was doubly tragic since she'd been pregnant when she'd died, and there had been too many losses in such a short period of time.

I smiled at him gently, and he managed to muster a bit of one in return for me as well. A great deal was communicated between us just then without a single word, and I went into the kitchen with my friends to make us all something to eat.

144

Hopefully, before long the power would be restored and we would be free, but in the meantime, we could eat, keep warm, wait for the light of day, and take the first chance we had to get out of there once and for all.

CHAPTER 18

"**T**HAT BACON SMELLS GREAT," HAZEL said as she hovered over the frying pan.

"Feel free to turn the pieces over while I work on the eggs," I said. I had decided to do a massive scramble so everyone could take as much or as little as they wanted.

"What, no donuts?" Jennifer asked with a smile.

"No donuts," I affirmed. "Frankly, I'm just not in the mood to make them or to eat them."

"I get that," she said softly. "What can I do to help?"

"Let's set up a buffet," I told her. "If you can get out plates, silverware, glasses, and napkins, folks can pick them up when they start through the line."

"I've got an idea. I'm going to get Elizabeth to help me," Jennifer said quietly. "She needs something to occupy her mind right now."

"I think that's a good idea," I said. "How is she doing?"

"She's in shock right now. Honestly, I think Henry is in worse shape than she is."

"I know she lost her husband, but he had to stand there helplessly while Cheyenne killed herself. That couldn't have been easy," I admitted.

"He keeps blaming himself," Jennifer said. "I'm worried about him."

"We won't be here forever," I told her. "Once we're free, he can get all of the help he needs."

After the impromptu breakfast was ready, I called out to the folks still in the living room, "Dinner is served. Grab a plate and help yourself."

Jake held back until he and I were the only two that hadn't been served yet. There was still a massive amount of food, and I wondered if we'd need it for later. I knew how power outages were. Sometimes they lasted just minutes or hours, but there were times they could last for days, and until we had electricity, we were stuck right where we were. "It looks great," he said as he helped himself to bacon and eggs. We had English muffins that I'd warmed in the oven, so I took one of those after Jake did and added a good amount of bacon and eggs to my plate as well. There was orange juice and coffee, so after I found a place for us to sit together away from the others, I came back for our drinks.

"This is really great," Jake said after taking a bite of scrambled eggs.

"It's nothing special," I said.

"I beg to differ. It's here, it's hot, and it's tasty," he answered with a grin. "Everybody else seems to be enjoying it, too."

I looked around and saw that he was right. As I started to scan the room, I realized that someone was missing.

As I put my plate down and stood, Jake asked me, "What's wrong?"

"Where's Henry?" I asked him softly. I'd seen him earlier, but he was now gone.

"I don't see him. Let's ask Lara," he suggested.

We found her searching the suites herself, and she was clearly startled when we ran into her. "Have either one of you seen my husband?" she asked us with a worried tone of voice.

"No," I said. "When was the last time you were with him?"

"I had to go to the restroom a few minutes ago, and when I got back, he was gone. I'm really worried about him. I've never seen him like this. He's falling apart."

"Don't discount what you've been through. After all, you saw her on the ledge, too," I reminded her. "You might not have seen her jump, but you were the next to the last person to see her before she died."

Lara frowned for a moment, and then she admitted, "That's not technically true. I was standing behind Henry when he opened the door. There was something in the way that was wedged against it, so it didn't open all the way up. He told me Cheyenne was on the ledge threatening to jump, but I never actually saw her."

That started a great many alarm bells ringing in my mind. "Did you at least hear their conversation?" I asked.

"No. Like I said, the door was jammed," Lara said. "Where could he be?"

"Did you check all of the bathrooms?" I asked her.

"No, just ours," she admitted.

"I'd go knock on every door if it were me," I said.

"I'll do that. Thanks."

"What are you up to?" Jake asked me the moment Lara was gone.

"We need to go back up on the roof," I said. "There's something I want to see."

"Care to share it with me?" he asked as he followed my lead.

"I'd rather be sure first," I admitted.

"Okay, that's good enough for me."

We managed to slip out without anyone noticing us, and after we climbed the stairs, I put my hand on the doorknob and told Jake, "Wait here for one second."

"Suzanne, you need to tell me what's going on."

"I just want to check something out," I said. "Keep the door partially closed."

He didn't look happy about it, but he did as I asked. I walked out onto the roof. It had gotten much more slippery than when we'd been up there earlier, and I had to really watch my step as I moved toward the edge where Cheyenne had fallen.

"Jake, can you hear me?" I asked in a normal voice.

Nothing.

"Jake?" I asked, raising my level just a smidge.

"What?" he asked as he came out the door. "Is something wrong?"

"Did you just hear me call your name?" I asked him.

"I thought I heard something the first time, but the second time I was sure. What's going on?" Then the light dawned in his eyes. "Henry was lying, wasn't he? Cheyenne didn't say a word to him when she saw him come out onto the roof. If she had, Lara would have heard it from where she was standing. Why would Henry lie about something like that?"

"I can think of one reason," I said as I looked around. If I was right, there had to be something within sight that might confirm my suspicion. I missed it at first, but after a moment, I saw something iced to the roof near the very edge. There was a massive duct of some kind close to it, and I had to wonder if it had pulled the paper into it before the freezing rain had a chance to accumulate. It was easy to crack the ice with the heel of my shoe, and as I pried it up, I heard a voice way too close to me saying, "I've been up here looking for that. I'll take it, if you don't mind."

And before I knew what was happening or could even react to his presence, I felt Henry's arm go around my throat as he started shoving me toward the edge of the roof, and sudden death.

All it would take were a few more steps, and I'd be on the ground below with Cheyenne.

She hadn't jumped any more than I would have.

I was sure of it.

Henry was the killer.

The only question I had was, why?

CHAPTER 19

"I'M CURIOUS ABOUT ONE THING. What gave me away?" he asked as he pressed his mouth toward my ear. He was so close I could smell bacon on his breath. Before I could answer though, he barked at Jake, "If you want her to die, by all means, go ahead and shoot me."

I looked over to see that my husband had trained his weapon on Henry's forehead. "Let my wife go, and I won't shoot you," Jake said, his voice calmer than I would have expected given the circumstances.

"I'm sorry, but that's just not going to happen. If you don't throw your weapon over the side, and I mean right now, I'm jumping, and I'm taking Suzanne with me."

Henry's grip was so tight across my throat that I knew that he was right. If he wanted to commit suicide, he would have no problem taking me with him over the edge.

"Don't throw your gun away, Jake. Go ahead and shoot him!" I knew if my husband sacrificed his weapon, our position would be worse than it was at the moment, if that was even possible.

"Suzanne, I'm sorry. I can't risk it," he said sadly. Before I could stop him, he chucked his handgun away from us all. It didn't fall off the edge, but it might as well have, given how far it skidded on the icy roof's surface.

"Why did you kill Cheyenne?" I asked Henry, trying to figure some way, any way, out of this. He might take me down with him, but I wasn't going to go without a fight. If I could keep him talking, I might just be able to come up with something, a plan that would somehow save me. Even if I couldn't, Jake was a smart man, and I had no doubt that he was trying to formulate something himself.

"I needed *someone* to take the fall for Jason's murder, and she seemed like the best candidate to me," Henry admitted. "That woman was a real hothead, and I knew folks wouldn't have any trouble believing that she killed her lover in a fit of rage after being rejected."

"How did you manage to get her up here in the first place?" Jake asked, distracting him a little to buy us both some time. I let one foot slip out a little from under me, and I felt my traction slip on the ice. If I'd had something to push against, I might be able to use it to my advantage, but what? There wasn't much around us besides the duct he'd hidden behind, but Henry was between it and me, so I couldn't use it at all. The only thing close to me was one of the banks of floodlights we'd seen lit up when we'd arrived. I wasn't sure they would be strong enough to withstand that kind of pressure, and it might just make the situation even worse.

Henry seemed almost pleased with himself as he explained, "I wrote her a note that said I had something of Jason's that I knew she'd want, something Elizabeth would never want her to have. Cheyenne actually loved that idiot, if you can believe it. It was almost too easy to lure her up here. She was holding the note in her hand, and as I grabbed for it before I pushed her, she pulled her hand back to keep me from getting it and started to slip. I had to take advantage of the opportunity, and one little nudge was all that it took. Unfortunately, I couldn't find the note before you all showed up. Lara came back with you all sooner than I'd expected."

"You put something in front of the door to stop us, didn't you?" Jake asked.

"I was trying to slow you down a little, but it didn't work," he admitted. "Now that I've got the note though, no one will be able to prove a thing. I'll ask you the same question one more time, Suzanne. What gave me away?"

I didn't see any harm in telling him. "You never mentioned her pregnancy. Cheyenne would have at least said something about it if she were leaving a verbal suicide note with you. The thing is, she told us earlier that she would have a part of Jason that no one could ever take from her. When I reflected on what she might have meant, I started to doubt that she would kill herself, but even if she did, she would have surely mentioned the baby to you."

"I honestly had no idea she was pregnant. I'll have to change my story when I retell it later. I'll explain it away by saying that I was so distraught at the time of her suicide, I wasn't thinking straight."

"Do you honestly think there's a chance you're getting out of this alive?" I asked him. "You had one of the strongest motives of anyone, though you let us all believe that your wife was the one upset about the failed investments. Even if that weren't true and *no one* suspected you, you might be able to kill me, but you'd never manage to shove Jake over the edge, too," I added, trying to keep him talking. Besides, what could it hurt pointing out the logic of the situation? He wasn't going to get away with the double murder now.

Unfortunately, my explanation only served to motivate him in a different direction. "You're right," he said, his shoulders slumping a little. "I'm finished. It was a good run, but I can see that it's nearing the end."

"Let her go, Henry," Jake ordered him. "Don't take her with you!"

"Why would I do that? Do you think my soul will burn any hotter if I have three victims on my head instead of two? If your wife hadn't meddled and dragged you up here, I would have gotten away with it. It's only fitting that she go down with me."

Things were going from bad to worse in a hurry. I had to think of something to say, anything to take his mind off killing himself and taking me with him. "Did you write the note Joan found?" I asked him.

"Yes, but it was obviously meant for Jason. I wanted him to suffer a little wondering which of his guests wanted to see him dead before I killed him. Jason ruined our lives, and I was going to make sure he paid for it. Then that simpering idiot Joan grabbed the note instead, so the threat was wasted on him. Lara demanded that I stand up to Jason, so I went to his suite the second I realized that he was alone. When I confronted him about our losses, he started laughing at me. He called me a gutless weasel! I started to leave, and that's when I saw the bookend. I was in a haze as I grabbed it and hit him! He stopped laughing, that was for sure."

"But then you panicked," I said, trying my best to brace myself if his grip loosened for a split second. If it did, I was determined to take advantage of it.

"Anybody would have done the same thing in my situation," Henry said. "That's enough talking. Let's get this over with. Say good-bye to your husband, Suzanne. You're about to take a little trip with me."

My time was running out! I decided that no matter what, I wasn't going to just give up! I dropped to my knees in one sudden motion, and just as I did, I saw Jake launch himself at Henry.

He wasn't holding back, and I was scared to death that his momentum would carry him over the side, along with the killer!

Reaching out with one hand to grab the base of the lights, I used the other to snag my husband's shirt as he zipped past me, a moment before he made impact with Henry Jackson.

Almost immediately I felt the material slip in my hand, and Jake continued his deadly path to the edge of the precipice along with the murderer.

Then, almost as though a miracle was happening, I managed to make one last grab for him. I missed his shirt, his belt, and even his pants, but I somehow managed to snag a shoe to stop him.

Henry wasn't so lucky.

As he went over the edge, I saw Jake lunge for the man's hand.

He had it for a second, but it slipped out of his grip.

I expected Henry to join his last victim on the pavement below, but he somehow managed to hang on to the edge.

"I've got you," Jake said a few seconds later as he pulled the killer back up on the roof with us. Apparently the man's survival instincts were stronger than he thought, because he did his best to hang on instead of just letting go when he had the chance. I wondered about the wisdom of saving the double killer, but I knew that it was the right thing to do. It wasn't up to us to act as judge and executioner. Let the courts deal with him.

At least this way, our hands and our consciences were clean.

"What happened?" Lara asked as we reentered the penthouse. "Why do you have my husband's hands tied up behind his back?"

She started toward him, but Jake stepped in between them before she could. "Henry killed Jason and Cheyenne," my husband said matter-of-factly.

"What? That's nonsense. Henry, tell them they've lost their minds," Lara said angrily.

"I'm not saying anything until I speak with an attorney," was the only thing that her husband would say.

"What? You don't need a lawyer unless you're guilty," she

said harshly. "Are you telling me that you did what they are accusing you of?"

Henry wanted to keep his mouth shut, you could see it in his eyes, and I knew that it was in his best interest to do just that, but he couldn't bring himself to do it. "Why are you acting so surprised all of a sudden? You've been filling my head with poisonous thoughts about him since we lost our life savings. How many times did you tell me that you wished that Jason were dead? Well, guess what, honey. Your wish came true tonight."

Lara seemed to crumple at the news. While it took the steam out of her anger, it only fueled Elizabeth's. She stepped forward, and before anyone could stop her, she slapped Henry so hard across the face that it left an imprint of her hand on his cheek.

"She hit me! You all saw it. I want her arrested for assault!" Henry protested.

"I'm sorry, but I didn't see anything," Jake said. "I was checking my watch, and I missed the entire thing. How about you, Suzanne?"

"I didn't see anything, either," I said with a smile.

When Elizabeth wound up to slap him again, I stepped in front of her. "If it happened again though, none of us would be able to deny seeing it. I don't think it would help matters anyway, do you?" I asked my friend gently.

"No. You're right."

"I'm so sorry for your loss," I repeated again to Elizabeth. "If I made things harder on you than they had to be, I'm sorry about that, too."

To my surprise and great relief, Elizabeth hugged me fiercely. As we shared the embrace, she whispered, "I'm sorry, too. You've been nothing but a good friend to me. Thank you for that."

"It was my pleasure," I said, glowing from the warmth of her forgiveness.

Henry wouldn't let the moment rest, though. "I want her arrested, and don't try to tell me that neither one of you saw it!"

"About that," Jake said. "I might have stretched the truth a bit when I said that I was deputized for life. It's more of an unspoken understanding than it is an official position of the department."

"Does that mean that I'm not really a deputy, either?" I asked him. That was too bad. I kind of liked being official for a change of pace.

"Sorry," my husband said with a grin.

"If you're not in law enforcement, then you have no right to restrain me," Henry said. "Untie my hands and set me free."

"It's all perfectly legal," Jake explained, making no move to undo the knots binding him. "I'm making a citizen's arrest. It will stand up in court, you don't have to worry about that."

"Why did he kill Cheyenne, though?" Joan asked, her voice little more than a whimper. "What did she ever do to him?"

"I'm standing right here," Henry said. "Ask me yourself."

"Why did you do it?" Joan asked, repeating the question.

"She was handy," Henry said with a simple shrug. His tone of voice was so casual that it gave me the chills. How could the man be so cold blooded? I could possibly understand the rage and passion that had driven him to kill Jason, but he'd lured Cheyenne to her death with promises that he had no intention or ability to keep. Maybe something had snapped in him when he'd murdered his best friend from childhood. The theory was troubling, but it was better than the alternative, that Henry had this streak of evil lying dormant for so many years that now was free.

"What do we do in the meantime?" Bernard asked. "I have pressing business elsewhere, and I really need to get out of here."

"Whatever it is, it's going to have to be without me," Candida replied icily.

"I assure you, we are finished," Bernard said, his voice so full of deadness that it caught me off guard.

"That's all I need to hear," she said.

"What do we do with him, Jake?" I asked my husband. "Should we lock him in the master closet of the main suite until the power comes back on?"

I hadn't been trying to keep my suggestion from Henry. "You can't put me in there with a dead man!"

"You know what? I think that's an excellent idea," Jake said.

Whether he was going to do it or not turned out to be a moot point.

Just then, the power came back on again, this time apparently for good.

It surged for a moment, the lights growing so bright that I was afraid the light bulbs might explode, and then it settled down to normal.

With that, everything came back on, including the cell phone boosters that we so desperately needed to call out for help.

Bernard headed straight for the door, but Jake stopped him. "Nobody's going anywhere until the police have arrived."

"You made a mistake just now by telling us you have no power here," Bernard said.

"I said I had no authority. I still have plenty of power to back it up, in case anyone wants to test me."

It was that hard cop voice that my husband used again, a tone that defied anyone to cross him.

Bernard certainly had no trouble realizing that Jake meant business. "Very well. Make your call, and gather your minions. I'll wait." With that, he took a seat away from the rest of us.

Jake nodded and then turned to everyone else. "Does anyone else have any complaints?"

There weren't any, so he pulled out his cell phone and made

the call he'd been wanting to make since we'd found Jason Martin's body.

Had it really been less than ten hours earlier? A great deal had happened in such a short time, and all I wanted to do right now was go back to our cottage in April Springs and forget that any of this had ever happened.

Unfortunately, knowing how the police operated in the case of a homicide, not to mention a double homicide, I knew that I wasn't going to be heading home for quite a while.

CHAPTER 20

"ARE YOU OKAY TO DRIVE?" Jake asked me as we pulled out of the parking lot. Dawn was just breaking, but at least the weather had taken a turn for the better. The ice and freezing rain had quickly melted under a warmer shower, and the sheen was already starting to leave the roadway. He'd called the state police instead of the local authorities, and we had all been interviewed and released in a decent amount of time.

"I'm fine. I can't wait to get back home though, can you?" I asked him.

"If it's all the same to you, I'd like to skip the next few party invitations we get," he said with a heavy sigh. "It was closer on that roof than I care to admit," he said. "I almost lost you."

"And then I almost lost you," I answered as I reached over and patted his knee. "Thanks for coming to my rescue."

"I was just about to say the same thing to you," he replied as he stifled a yawn.

"You can take a nap on the way back if you'd like," I told him.

"Why aren't you more tired than you are?"

"This is early for most folks, but I'm usually working at this time of day anyway."

"You're not the least bit sleepy after staying up all night?"

"Don't get me wrong. The second we get back to the cottage, I want to light a fire and hit the couch for a nice long nap."

"We could always go back to bed when we get home," Jake suggested.

"It would feel too decadent," I admitted. "Besides, I just love the radiant heat of the fireplace. It makes the cold weather worth experiencing, don't you think?"

"All I need is you," he said with a grin. "If you're awake, then so am I."

"It's your call," I said. "I've got to rest up while I can. In three days, Emma is taking a two-week leave of absence to help Barton with his restaurant launch."

"Do you need me to help you out at the donut shop while she's gone?" he asked, the dread obvious in his voice.

"No, I've got it covered. Sharon's coming in, so you're off the hook."

"That sounds good to me," he said.

"You know, it's amazing how many people wanted to see harm come to Jason. On paper it appeared that he had everything: a successful business, a loving wife, standing in the community, all of it, but when it came down to it, he didn't have *anything*."

Jake didn't respond, and when I glanced over at him, I saw that he was asleep despite his best intentions.

I didn't mind. He'd earned it, and more.

I might not have owned anything close to what some of the other couples had that we'd been with over the past day, but I had a job I loved, a husband I adored, friends and family I could count on, and what was more, they knew that they could count on me, too.

It was more than enough for me, and as I drove back to April Springs, I realized just how good it felt to be going home again.

RECICES

Basic Chocolate Donuts

This is a decent chocolate donut recipe when you're in the mood for a fried cocoa treat. They're a little heavy, especially compared to some of my other donuts, but we like them as a change of pace. For an extra kick, mix a packet of instant hot cocoa in with the batter to give it a little more pizzazz. A friend of mine bumps it up a notch and uses the packet as a dusting on top after glazing the donut lightly, but do so at your own risk; it's a little too much chocolate for my taste! You can also try icing these with a store-bought canned product if you'd like a little more sweetness, but any way you try these, they're good!

Ingredients

- 1 egg, beaten
- 1/2 cup sugar
- 1 tablespoon butter, melted
- 1 tablespoon cinnamon
- 1/2 cup whole milk
- 1/4 cup bittersweet chocolate, melted
- 2 cups all-purpose flour
- 1 teaspoon baking powder

Optional

- 1 to 2 packets instant hot cocoa mix

- 1 can icing (approx. 16 oz.)

Directions

Heat enough oil in a pan to cover the donuts at 370 degrees F.

While the oil is coming to temperature, take a medium-sized bowl and beat the egg, add the sugar, butter, cinnamon, and milk, and then gradually add the melted chocolate, gently stirring the entire time. In a smaller bowl, sift together the flour and baking powder, then slowly add the dry mix to the wet, again stirring gently. Roll the dough out to ¼ inch thickness and then cut out your donut shapes.

Let them rest a few minutes, and then add them gradually to the hot oil for four to five minutes, flipping them over halfway through the process.

Then top them however you'd like, including with the optional canned icing or hot cocoa powder mix, and enjoy!

Makes 6 to 8 donuts.

Chocolate Peanut Butter Cookie Delights

I've loved these cookies since I was a kid, and age hasn't done a thing to dull my enthusiasm for them. My favorite way to eat them is soon after they are out of the oven, with the chocolate on top still soft, but if you want to come close to the experience after you've frozen them, microwave them carefully until the chocolate begins to melt again. Some folks can't tell the difference from fresh cookies prepared that way, but in my opinion, nothing beats them fresh out of the oven!

Ingredients

- 1 cup unsalted butter, softened
- 3/4 cup brown sugar
- 3/4 cup granulated sugar
- 1 teaspoon vanilla extract
- 2 eggs, beaten
- 1 cup peanut butter, chunky or smooth
- 3 cups flour
- 2 teaspoons baking soda
- 1/8 teaspoon salt
- Enough Hershey's Kisses™ to top each cookie, about 1 bag

Directions

Preheat the oven to 375 degrees F.

Take a large bowl and cream together the butter, brown sugar, white sugar, and vanilla extract until it is thoroughly mixed together. Next, beat the eggs and add them to the mix. Then follow with the peanut butter, incorporating it into the mix as well. In a separate bowl, sift the flour, baking soda, and salt, and then gradually add it to the wet mix, stirring as you go.

Pinch off pieces of dough the size of your thumb and place them on an ungreased cookie sheet or parchment paper, which is my personal preference. Bake them 8 to 10 minutes or until they are nearly done (it's a bit of an art to judge exactly when this is, but you get the hang of it fairly quickly). Pull the sheet out of the oven and place one chocolate goodie on top of each cookie, then return to the oven to finish baking. The chocolate will get a bit soft, but it should retain its shape.

Remove from the rack, let cool as long as your willpower allows, and then enjoy!

Makes 24 to 36 cookies.

Baked Chocolate Perfection Donuts

This is the donut recipe for the true chocolate lover. I've been making these for years, and I keep coming up with new ideas on how to dress them up and enhance them, but the gang still loves the original version the best.

Ingredients

Dry
- 1 cup unbleached all-purpose flour (not self-rising)
- 1/4 cup cocoa (unsweetened)
- 1 teaspoon baking powder
- 1/4 teaspoon baking soda
- 1/4 teaspoon cinnamon
- 1/4 teaspoon nutmeg
- 1/8 teaspoon salt

Wet
- 1 large egg or two medium ones, beaten
- 1/2 cup chocolate milk (2% or whole preferred)
- 3 tablespoons unsalted butter, melted
- 1/2 cup granulated sugar
- 1 teaspoon vanilla extract

Directions

Preheat your oven to 350 degrees F.

In a large bowl, sift together the flour, cocoa, baking powder, baking soda, cinnamon, nutmeg, and salt. In a different bowl, combine the wet ingredients, starting with the beaten egg, then following up with the chocolate milk, melted butter, sugar, and vanilla extract. Mix together well, and then slowly add the wet ingredients to the dry, mixing it in gently. If you over-mix at this stage, your donuts may be denser and chewier than you might like, so a gentle hand is needed here.

Place the batter in a donut mold or use lined cupcake trays if you'd like.

Bake 6 to 7 minutes or until the donuts spring back from a light touch, but be careful—they're really hot at this point!

Remove the donuts and cool on a tray.

Top with chocolate icing from a can or make your own glaze.

Makes 5 to 9 donuts.

The Best Hot Chocolate In The World

Okay, I might be exaggerating a little, but not by much, at least according to my family. We go so far as to make big batches during the holiday season and give jars of the mix as presents! If you do this, some mini marshmallows on top really add to the presentation. The bonus about this mix is that it's easy to make and yet still has a flavor that far exceeds what you can buy at the store, at least according to my clan.

Ingredients

- 2 cups nonfat dry powdered milk
- 3/4 cup granulated sugar
- 1/2 cup Special Dark Hershey's Cocoa, Dutch processed powder
- 1/2 cup Hershey's Cocoa, natural unsweetened powder
- 1/2 cup powdered non-dairy creamer
- A dash of salt

Directions

Take a large mixing bowl and combine the powdered milk, granulated sugar, Dutch cocoa, unsweetened cocoa, powdered creamer, and salt.

Mix thoroughly and you're finished! I told you it was easy.

When you are ready for your first cup, take 1/4 cup of the mix, add it to your favorite mug, and then add 3/4 cup hot milk. Stir until the powder is dissolved and add mini marshmallows if you are so inclined.

Makes 4 1/4 cups of mix.

I won't even try to estimate how many cups of hot cocoa this produces, since everyone in my family uses the suggested ¼ cup of mix more as a suggestion than a firm requirement. Some like it stronger, and some prefer a less robust taste to their hot cocoa. Feel free to experiment until you find the ratio of mix to milk that's just right for you!

If you enjoy Jessica Beck Mysteries and you would like to be notified when the next book is being released, please visit our website at jessicabeckmysteries.net for valuable information about Jessica's books, and sign up for her new-releases-only mail blast.

Your email address will not be shared, sold, bartered, traded, broadcast, or disclosed in any way. There will be no spam from us, just a friendly reminder when the latest book is being released, and of course, you can drop out at any time.

OTHER BOOKS BY JESSICA BECK

A Baked Ham
A Bad Egg
A Real Pickle
A Burned Biscuit

The Ghost Cat Cozy Mysteries
Ghost Cat: Midnight Paws
Ghost Cat 2: Bid for Midnight

The Cast Iron Cooking Mysteries
Cast Iron Will
Cast Iron Conviction
Cast Iron Alibi
Cast Iron Motive
Cast Iron Suspicion

Made in the USA
Columbia, SC
18 December 2017